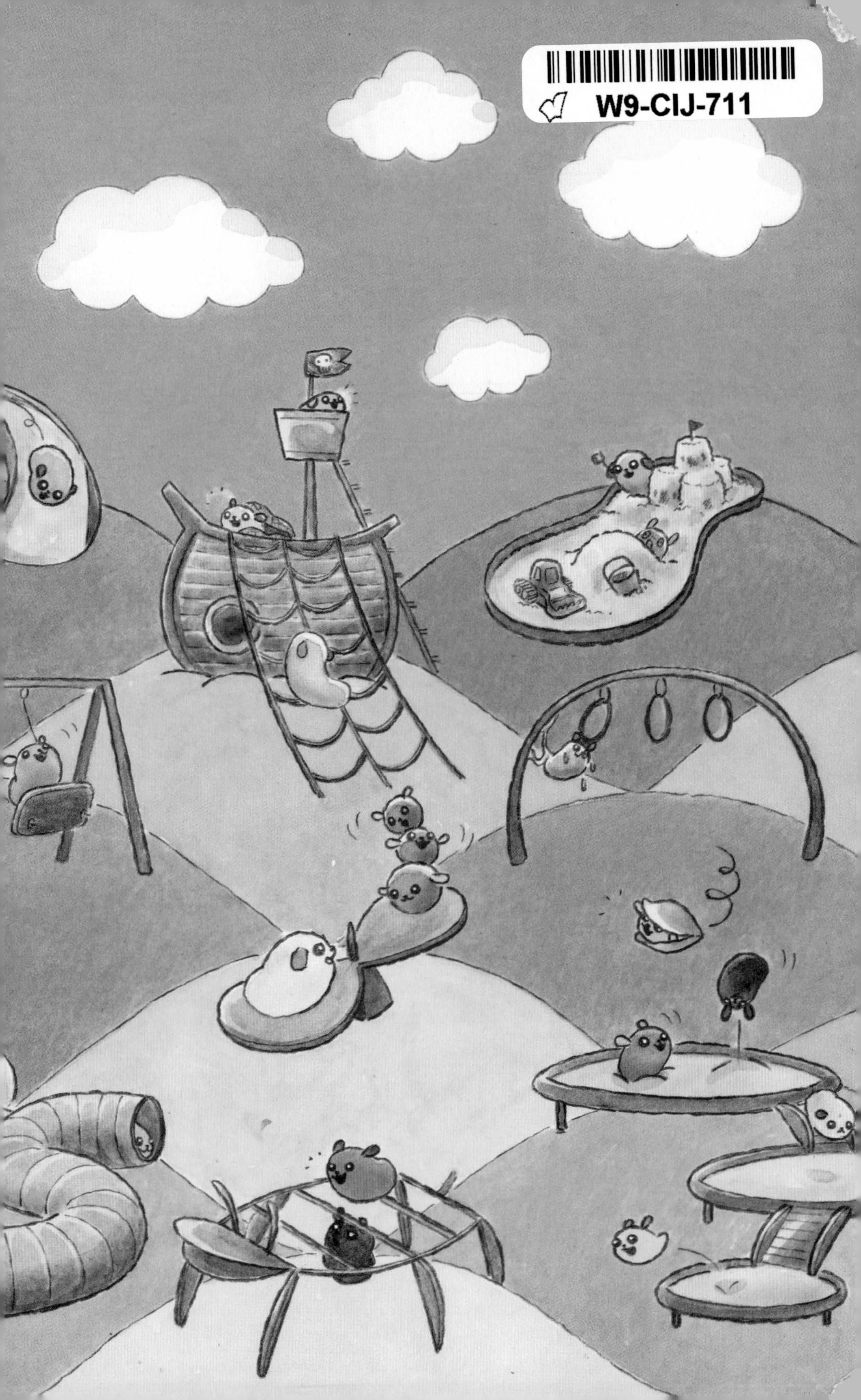

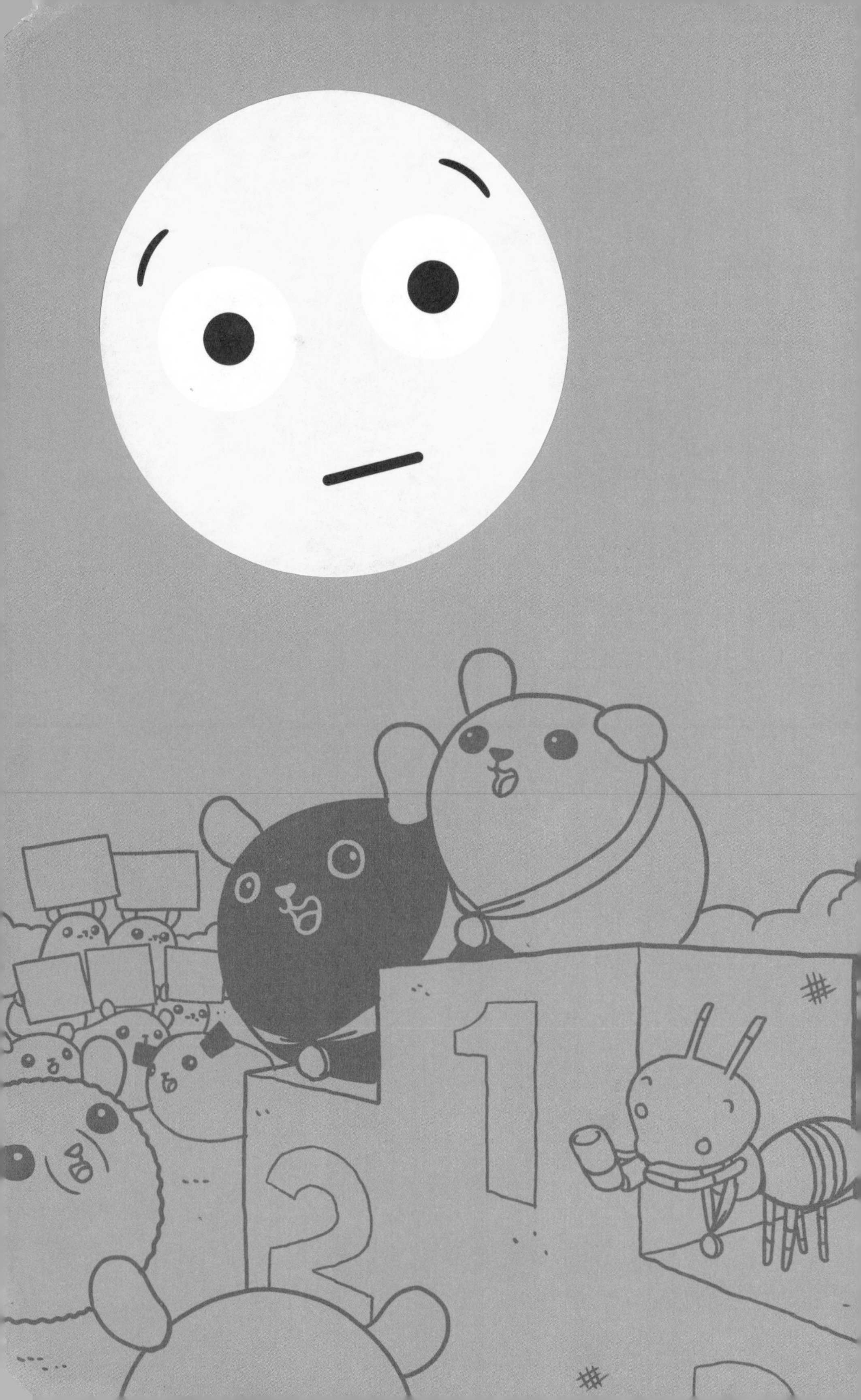
2
1

mameshiba

We Could Be HEROES!

stories by
james turner

art by
jorge monlongo

"Mameshiba Shorts" by
lark pien

Mameshiba: We Could Be Heroes!

Stories by **James Turner**
Art by **Jorge Monlongo**
Endpapers and "Mameshiba Shorts" by **Lark Pien**

Cover Art • **Jorge Monlongo**
Graphics and Cover Design • **Fawn Lau**
Editor • **Traci N. Todd**
Original Mameshiba Character Creation and Design • **Sukwon Kim**
Original Mameshiba Art Direction • **Shoko Watanabe**

Special thanks to Chris Duffy for his support and guidance.

Printed in China

Published by VIZ Media, LLC
P.O. Box 77010
San Francisco, CA 94107

10 9 8 7 6 5 4 3 2 1
First printing, July 2012

www.vizkids.com
www.viz.com

RATED A FOR ALL AGES
PARENTAL ADVISORY
MAMESHIBA: WE COULD BE HEROES! is rated A and is suitable for readers of all ages.
ratings.viz.com

Table of Contents

What are Mameshiba?

Simply put, *mameshiba* means "bean dog" in Japanese. But Mameshiba aren't beans or dogs. They're a little bit of both! And the one thing these bean dogs like more than anything else is trivia. So if you ever see a Mameshiba and it asks, "Did you know?" listen up. Because you're about to hear something very special.

Edamame

Edamame is the brave, determined leader of the pack.

Red Bean

Red Bean is sharp, polite, very popular little bean.

Boiled Bean

Boiled Bean is a caring, helpful bean who's always just a little moist.

Chickpea

Chickpea hates to be left out and can be a wee bit self-involved.

Peanut

Peanut likes to try new things and always thinks outside the shell.

Black Soybean

Black Soybean is the athlete of the bunch.

Lentil

Lentil is aware of everything that's going on and is passionate about facts and figures.

Lima Bean

Lima Bean is a know-it-all who doesn't know that being a know-it-all is annoying.

Sweet Beans

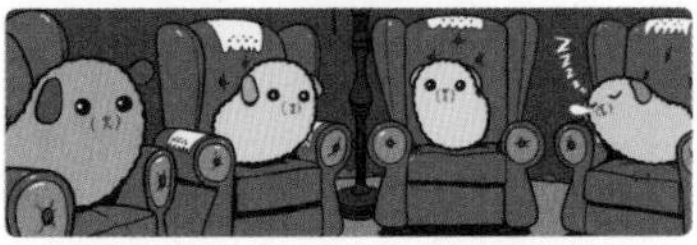

The Sweet Beans are very old and very wise.

Pistachio

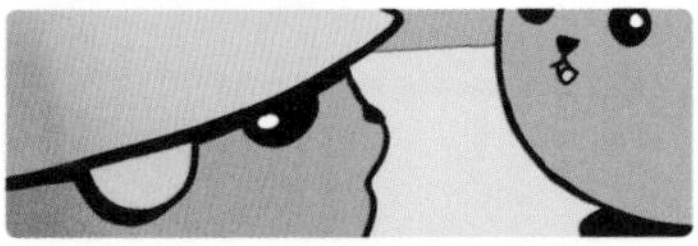

Pistachio is the quiet, hide-in-the-shell type.

Chili Bean

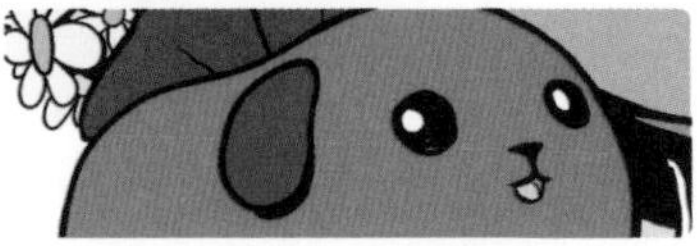

Chili Bean is a true romantic.

Almond

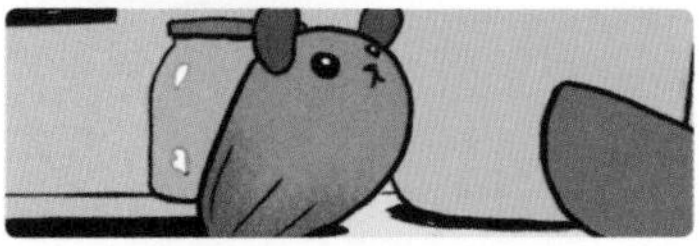

Almond's a bit uptight and is Cocoa Bean's best friend.

Natto

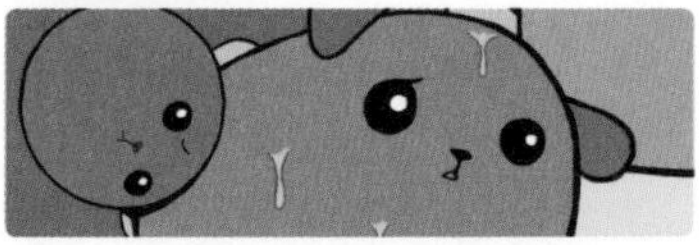

Natto always sticks to its guns. And just about everything else.

Black-Eyed Pea

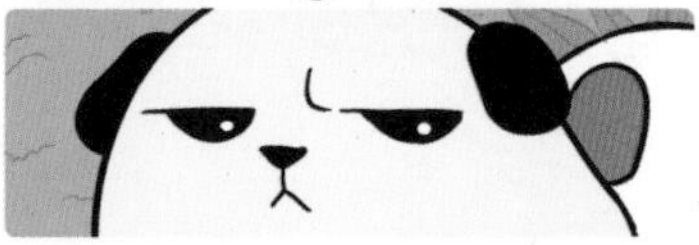

Black-Eyed Pea is a cool legume with a very dry sense of humor.

Black Bean

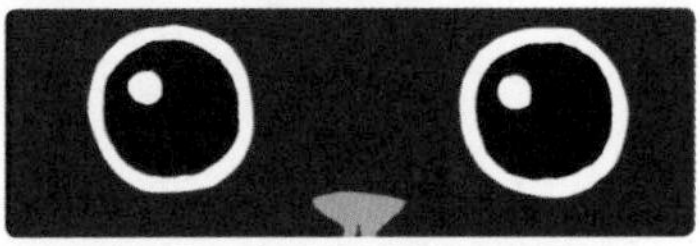

Black Bean is very shy and has perfected the fine art of staring.

Tiger Bean

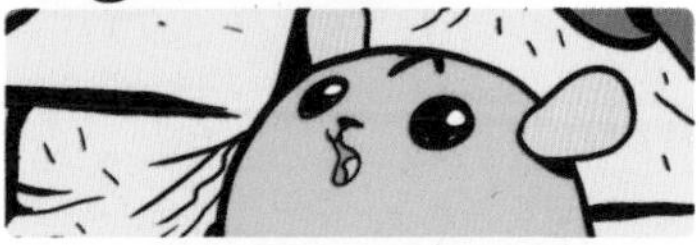

Tiger is a forgetful little bean who can sometimes be a bit selfish.

White Soybean

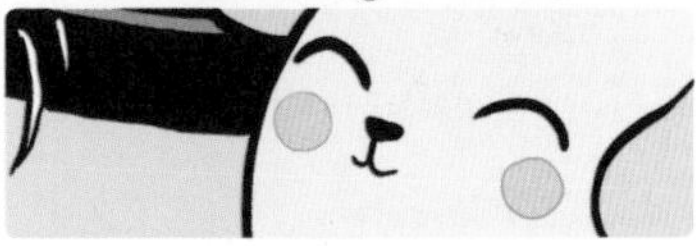

White Soybean's heart is pure and true.

Cocoa Bean

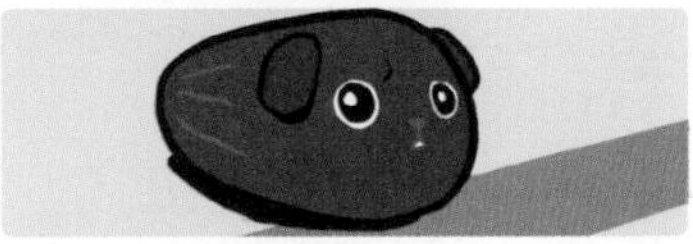

Cocoa has a wide-eyed, innocent view of the world.

Cranberry Bean

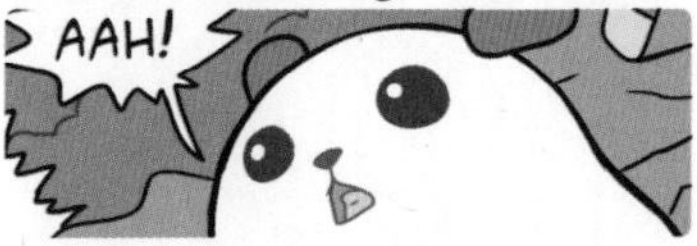
AAH!

Cranberry is very competitive and wants to be the best at everything.

The Scream

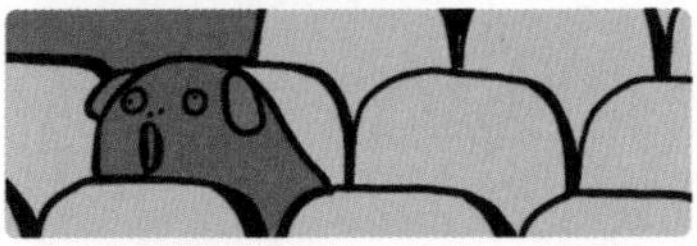

This mysterious bean is rarely ever seen, but it's hiding in this book. Can you find it?

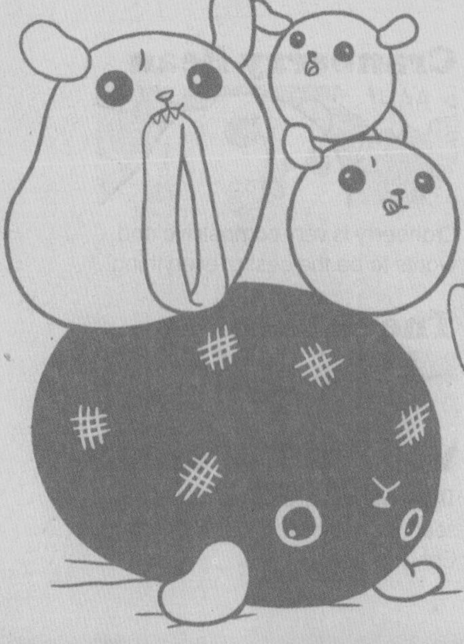

mameshiba

We Could Be HEROES!

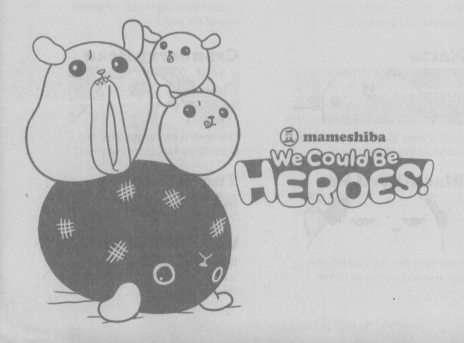

CHILI BEAN in Love

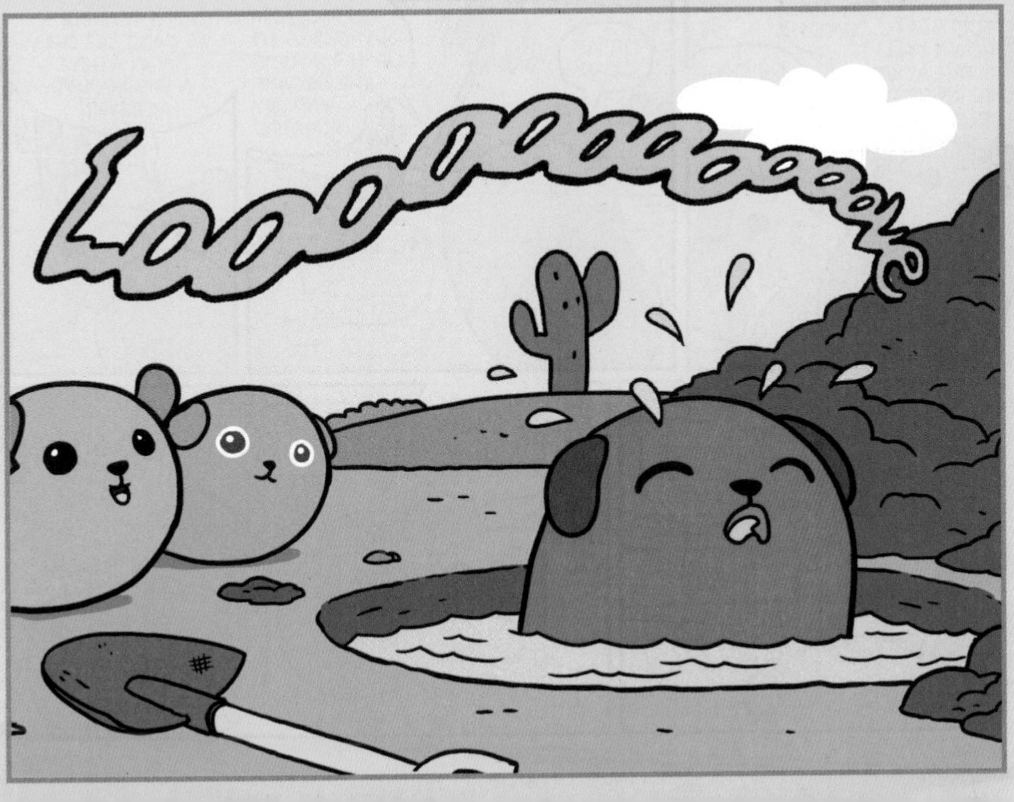
Looooooooooooove

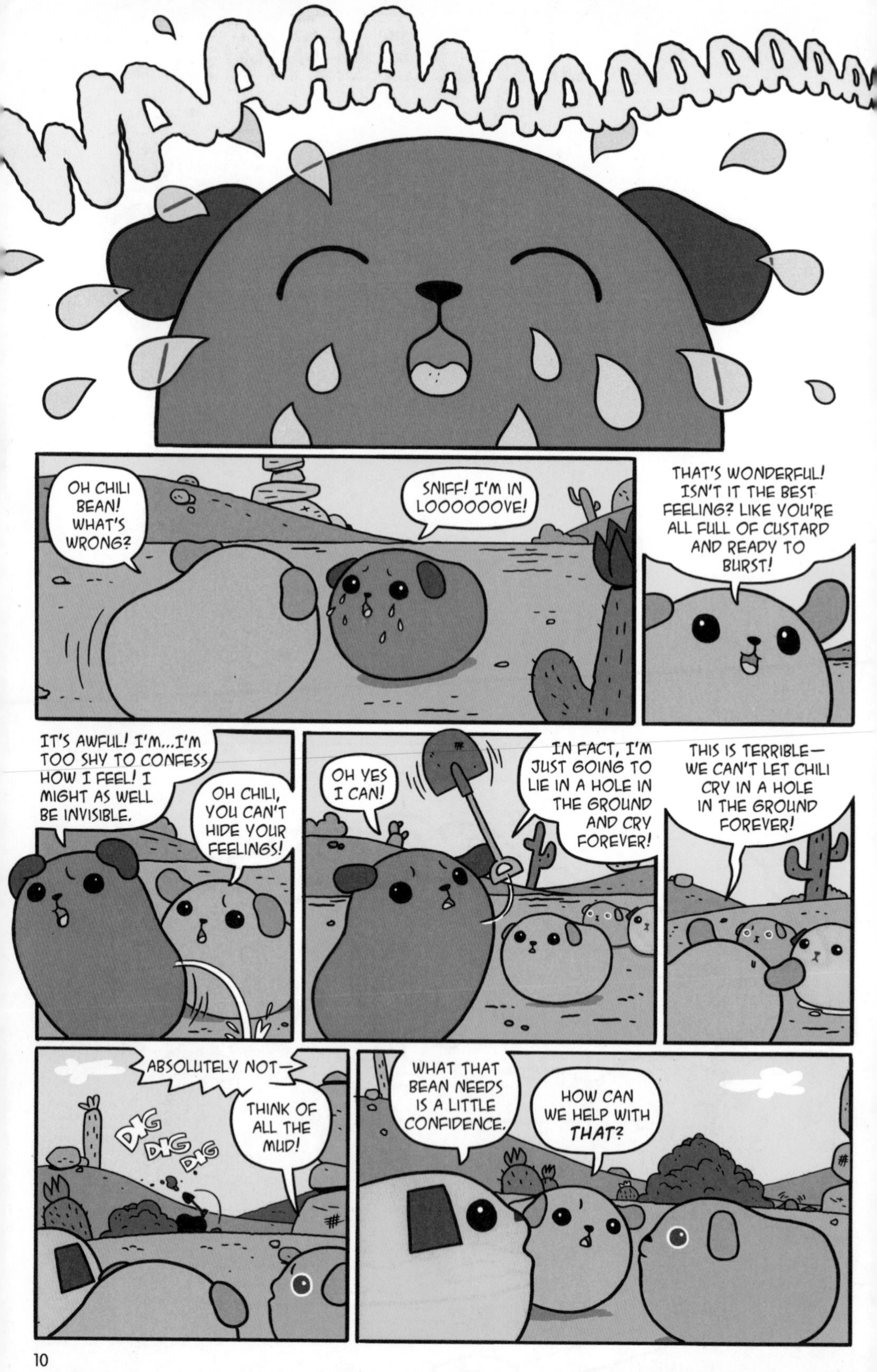
WAAAAAAAAAAAA
OH CHILI BEAN! WHAT'S WRONG?
SNIFF! I'M IN LOOOOOOVE!
THAT'S WONDERFUL! ISN'T IT THE BEST FEELING? LIKE YOU'RE ALL FULL OF CUSTARD AND READY TO BURST!
IT'S AWFUL! I'M...I'M TOO SHY TO CONFESS HOW I FEEL! I MIGHT AS WELL BE INVISIBLE.
OH CHILI, YOU CAN'T HIDE YOUR FEELINGS!
OH YES I CAN!
IN FACT, I'M JUST GOING TO LIE IN A HOLE IN THE GROUND AND CRY FOREVER!
THIS IS TERRIBLE— WE CAN'T LET CHILI CRY IN A HOLE IN THE GROUND FOREVER!
ABSOLUTELY NOT—
DIG DIG DIG
THINK OF ALL THE MUD!
WHAT THAT BEAN NEEDS IS A LITTLE CONFIDENCE.
HOW CAN WE HELP WITH THAT?

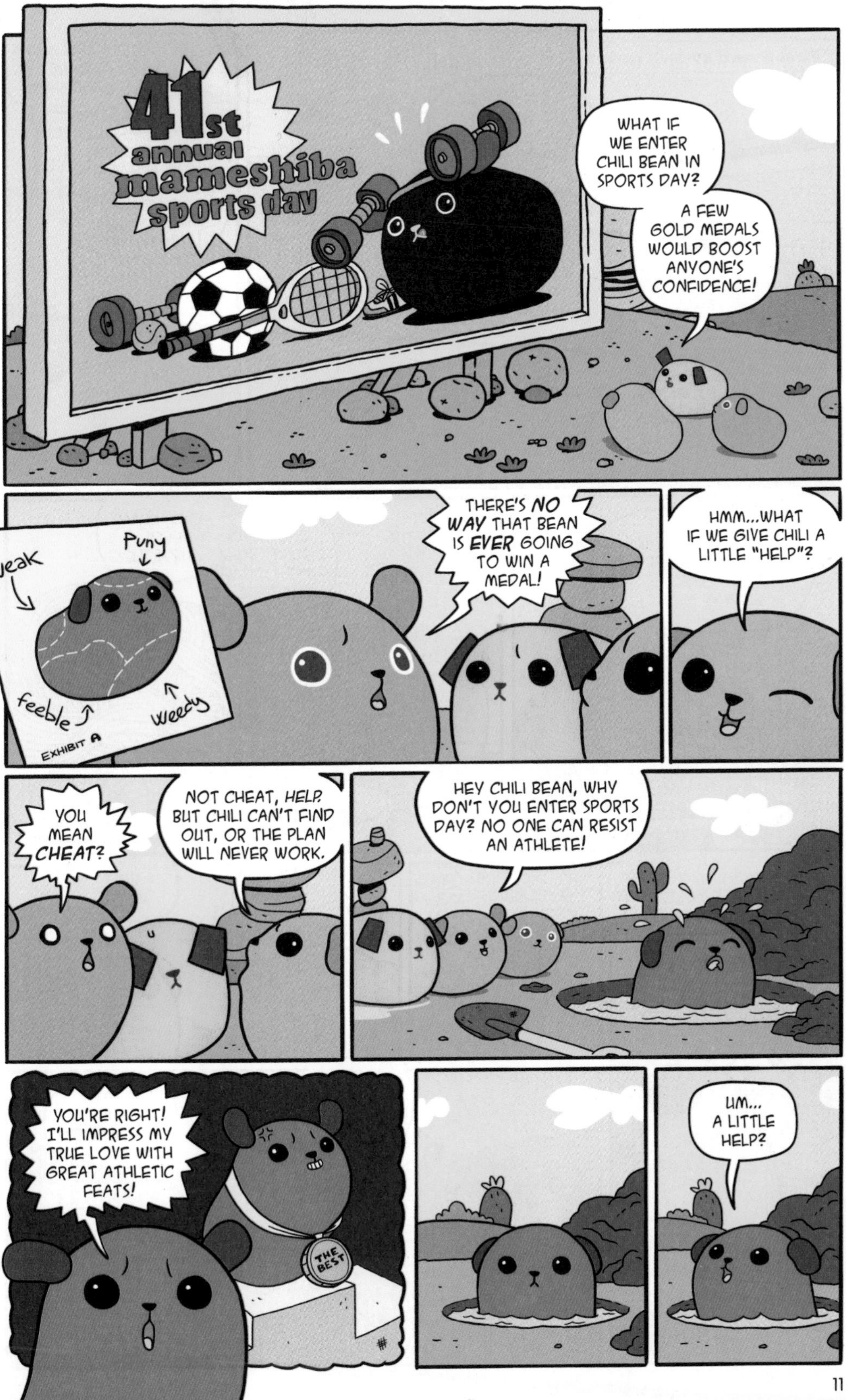

41st annual mameshiba sports day
WHAT IF WE ENTER CHILI BEAN IN SPORTS DAY?
A FEW GOLD MEDALS WOULD BOOST ANYONE'S CONFIDENCE!
Puny
weak
feeble
weedy
EXHIBIT A
THERE'S NO WAY THAT BEAN IS EVER GOING TO WIN A MEDAL!
HMM...WHAT IF WE GIVE CHILI A LITTLE "HELP"?
YOU MEAN CHEAT?
NOT CHEAT, HELP. BUT CHILI CAN'T FIND OUT, OR THE PLAN WILL NEVER WORK.
HEY CHILI BEAN, WHY DON'T YOU ENTER SPORTS DAY? NO ONE CAN RESIST AN ATHLETE!
YOU'RE RIGHT! I'LL IMPRESS MY TRUE LOVE WITH GREAT ATHLETIC FEATS!
THE BEST
UM... A LITTLE HELP?

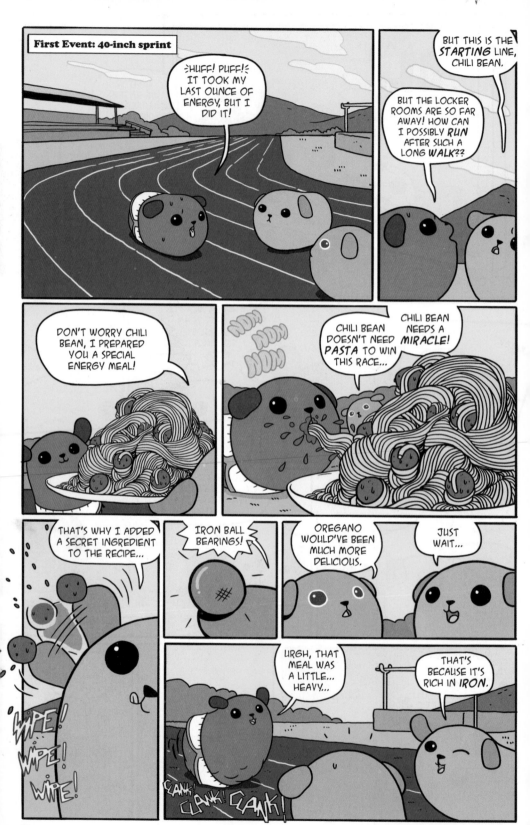

First Event: 40-inch sprint

:HUFF! PUFF!: IT TOOK MY LAST OUNCE OF ENERGY, BUT I DID IT!

BUT THIS IS THE *STARTING* LINE, CHILI BEAN.

BUT THE LOCKER ROOMS ARE SO FAR AWAY! HOW CAN I POSSIBLY *RUN* AFTER SUCH A LONG *WALK*??

DON'T WORRY CHILI BEAN, I PREPARED YOU A SPECIAL ENERGY MEAL!

NOM NOM NOM

CHILI BEAN DOESN'T NEED *PASTA* TO WIN THIS RACE...

CHILI BEAN NEEDS A *MIRACLE!*

THAT'S WHY I ADDED A SECRET INGREDIENT TO THE RECIPE...

IRON BALL BEARINGS!

OREGANO WOULD'VE BEEN MUCH MORE DELICIOUS.

JUST WAIT...

WIPE! WIPE! WIPE!

URGH, THAT MEAL WAS A LITTLE... HEAVY...

THAT'S BECAUSE IT'S RICH IN *IRON.*

CLANK! CLANK! CLANK!

12

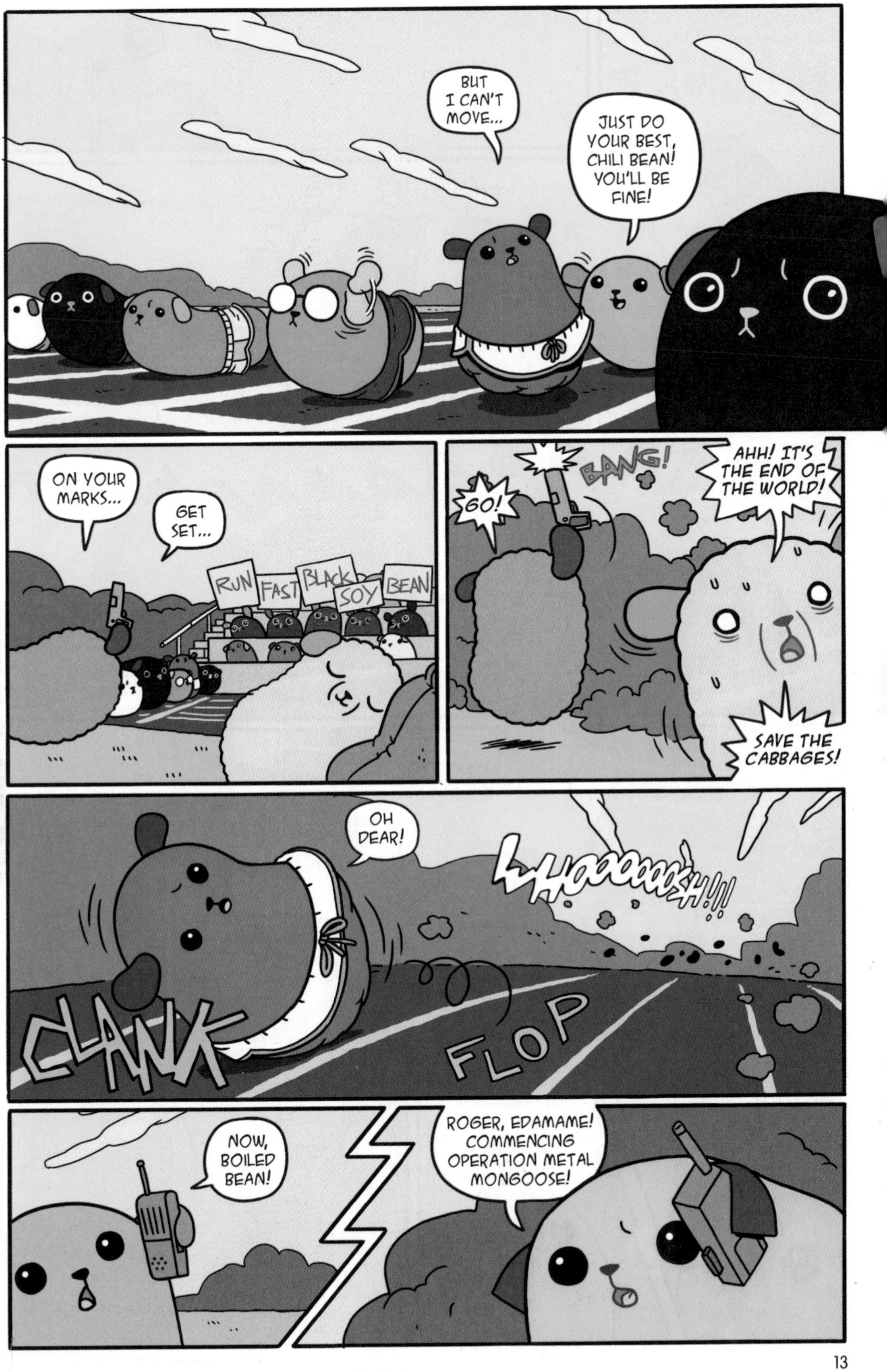
BUT I CAN'T MOVE...
JUST DO YOUR BEST, CHILI BEAN! YOU'LL BE FINE!
ON YOUR MARKS...
GET SET...
RUN
FAST
BLACK
SOY
BEAN
GO!
BANG!
AHH! IT'S THE END OF THE WORLD!
SAVE THE CABBAGES!
OH DEAR!
WHOOOOOOSH!!!
CLANK
FLOP
NOW, BOILED BEAN!
ROGER, EDAMAME! COMMENCING OPERATION METAL MONGOOSE!

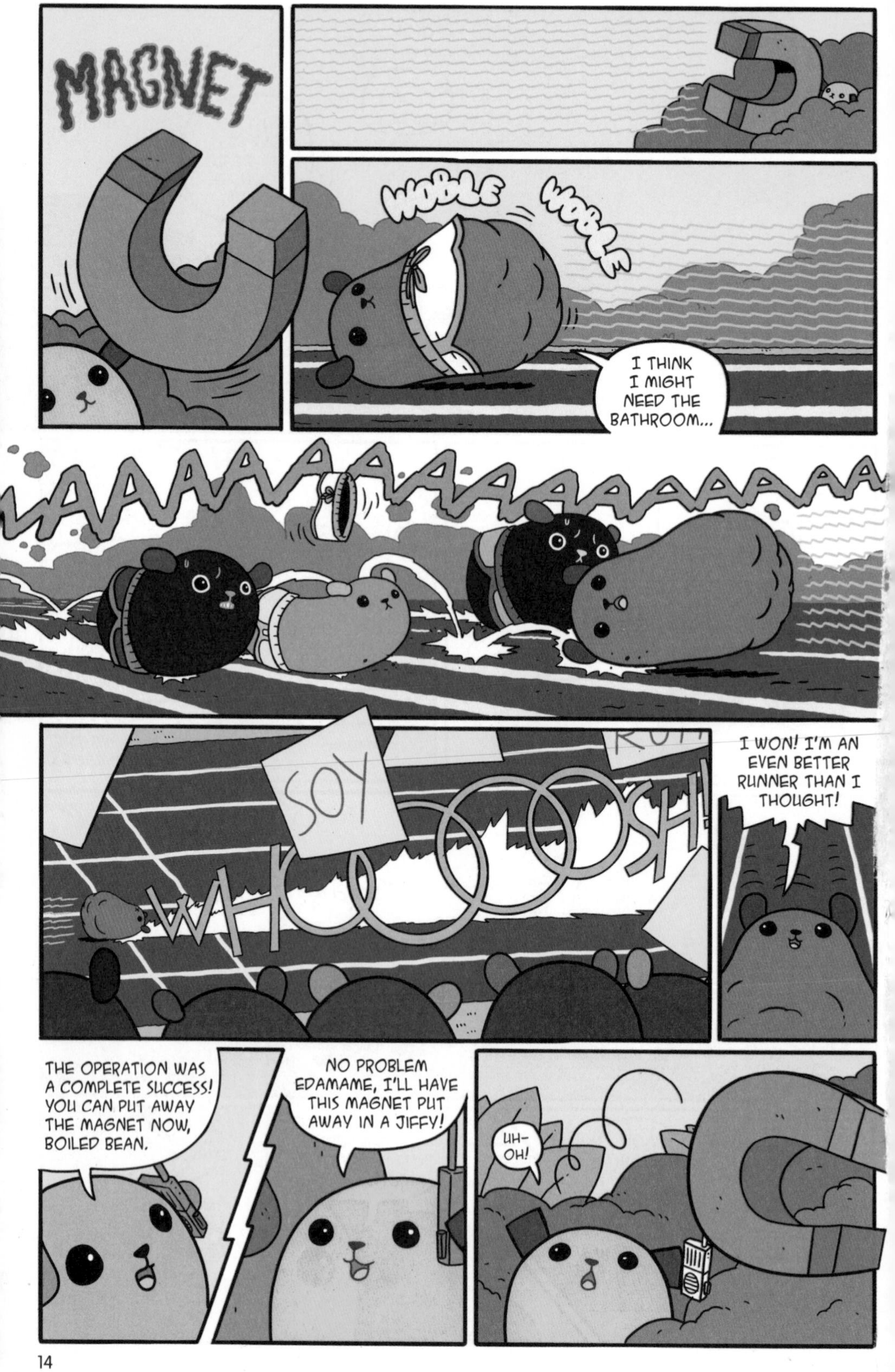
MAGNET
WOBLE
WOBLE
I THINK I MIGHT NEED THE BATHROOM...
AAAAAAAAAAAAAAAA
SOY
WHOOOOOSH!
I WON! I'M AN EVEN BETTER RUNNER THAN I THOUGHT!
THE OPERATION WAS A COMPLETE SUCCESS! YOU CAN PUT AWAY THE MAGNET NOW, BOILED BEAN.
NO PROBLEM EDAMAME, I'LL HAVE THIS MAGNET PUT AWAY IN A JIFFY!
UH-OH!

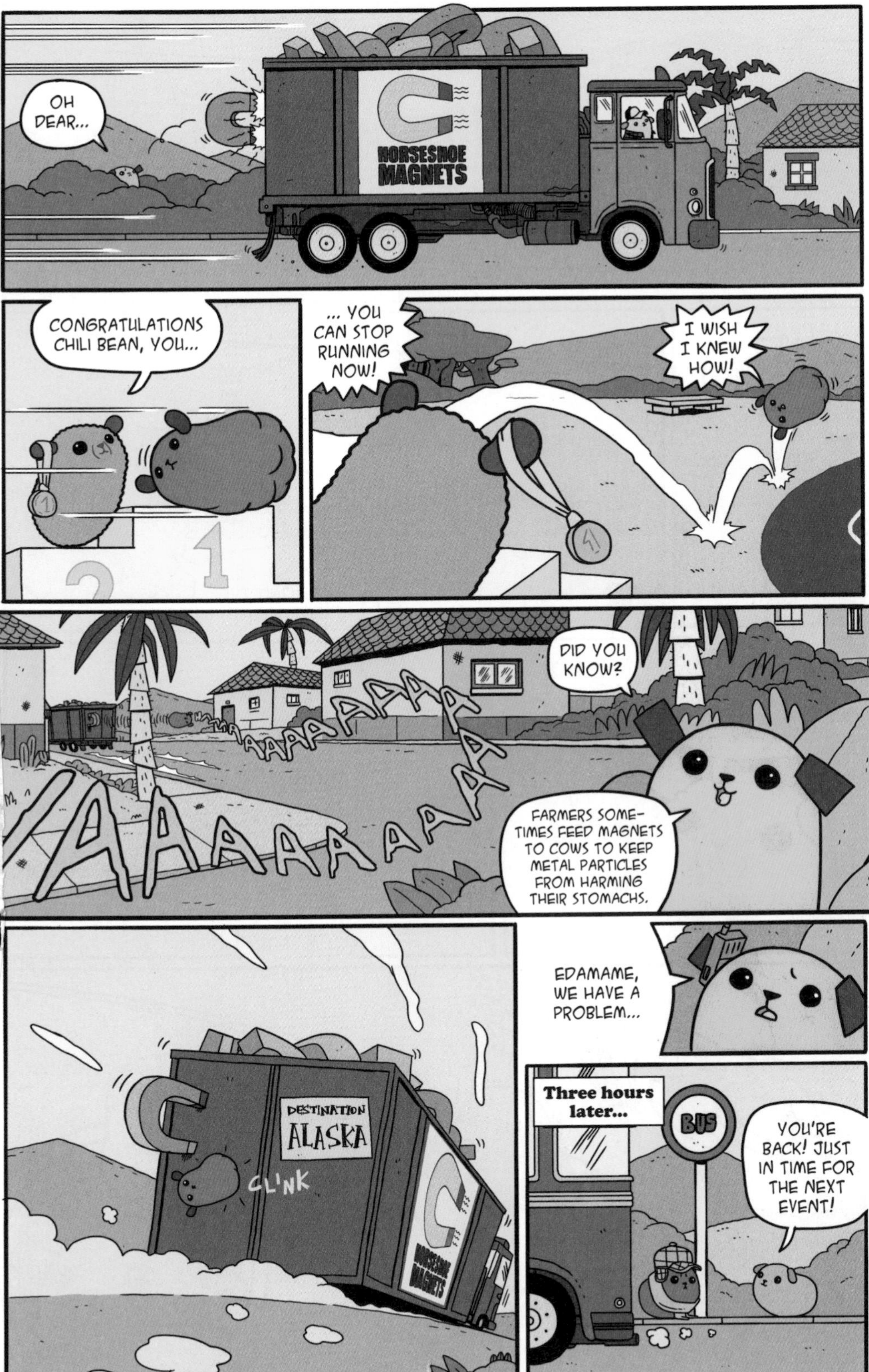
OH DEAR...
HORSESHOE MAGNETS
CONGRATULATIONS CHILI BEAN, YOU...
... YOU CAN STOP RUNNING NOW!
I WISH I KNEW HOW!
AAAAAAAAAAAAAAAAAAAAA
DID YOU KNOW?
FARMERS SOMETIMES FEED MAGNETS TO COWS TO KEEP METAL PARTICLES FROM HARMING THEIR STOMACHS.
DESTINATION ALASKA
CLINK
HORSESHOE MAGNETS
EDAMAME, WE HAVE A PROBLEM...
Three hours later...
BUS
YOU'RE BACK! JUST IN TIME FOR THE NEXT EVENT!

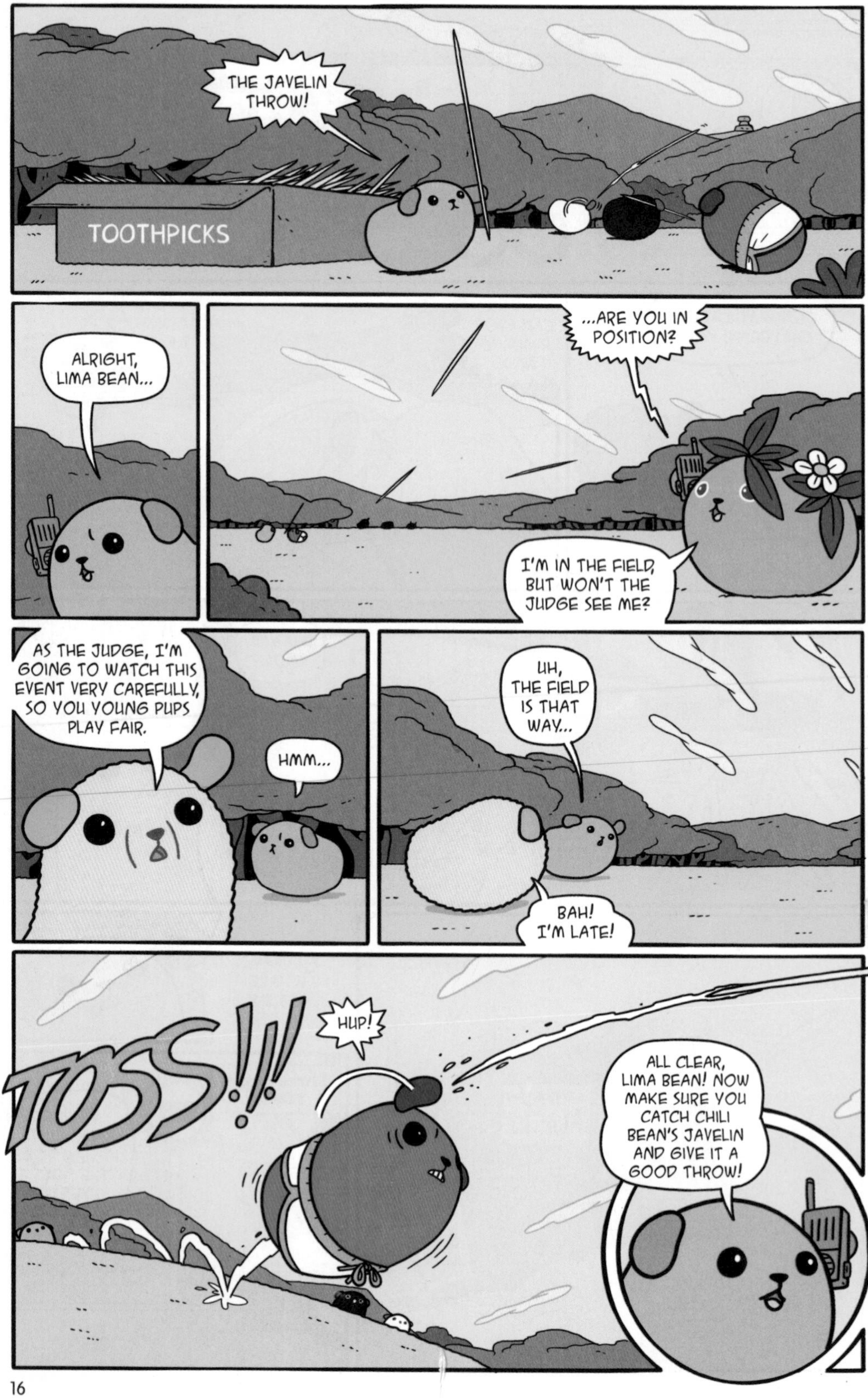
THE JAVELIN THROW!
TOOTHPICKS
ALRIGHT, LIMA BEAN...
...ARE YOU IN POSITION?
I'M IN THE FIELD, BUT WON'T THE JUDGE SEE ME?
AS THE JUDGE, I'M GOING TO WATCH THIS EVENT VERY CAREFULLY, SO YOU YOUNG PUPS PLAY FAIR.
HMM...
UH, THE FIELD IS THAT WAY...
BAH! I'M LATE!
TOSS!!!
HUP!
ALL CLEAR, LIMA BEAN! NOW MAKE SURE YOU CATCH CHILI BEAN'S JAVELIN AND GIVE IT A GOOD THROW!

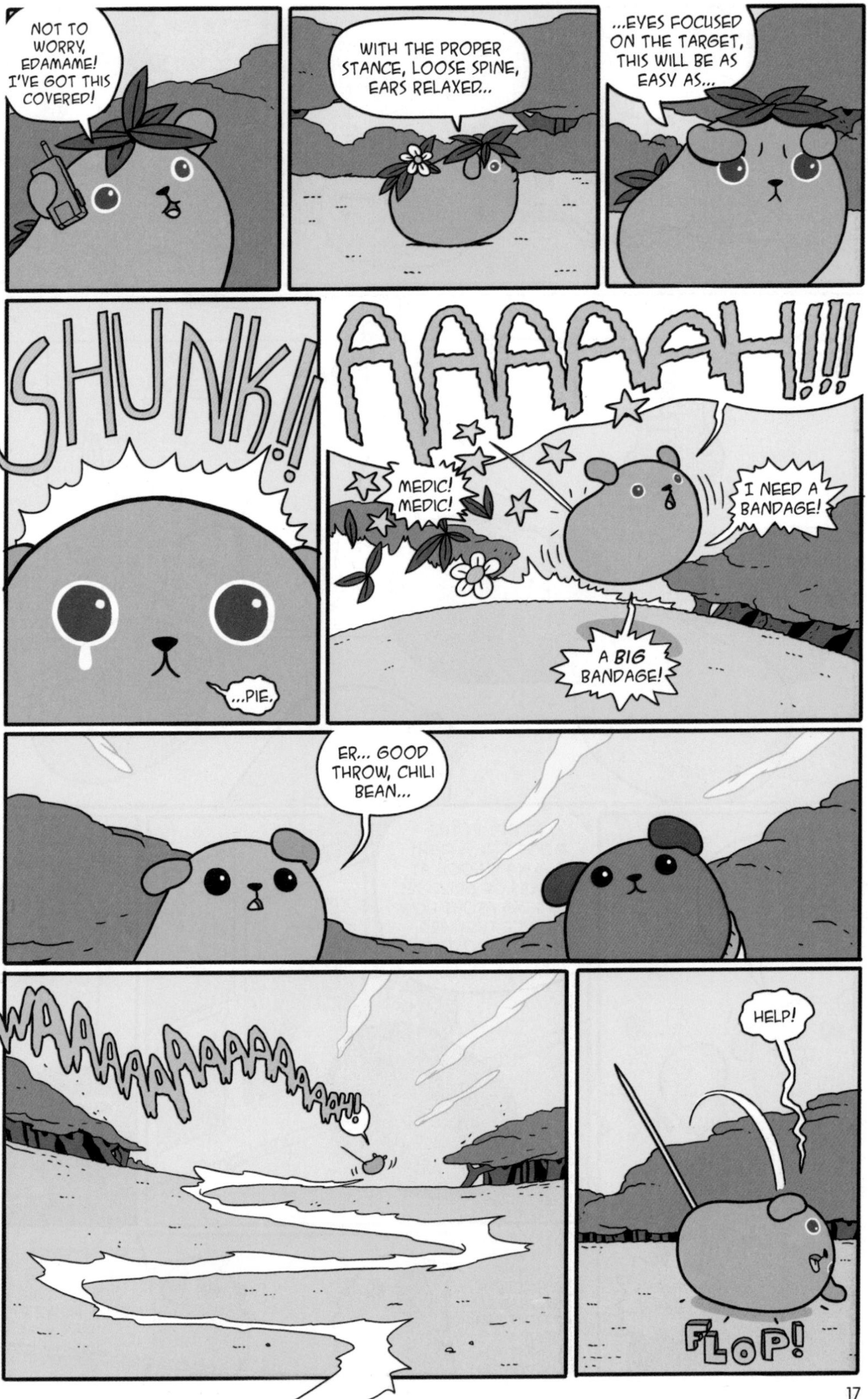
NOT TO WORRY, EDAMAME! I'VE GOT THIS COVERED!
WITH THE PROPER STANCE, LOOSE SPINE, EARS RELAXED...
...EYES FOCUSED ON THE TARGET, THIS WILL BE AS EASY AS...
SHUNK!!
...PIE.
AAAAAH!!!
MEDIC! MEDIC!
I NEED A BANDAGE!
A BIG BANDAGE!
ER... GOOD THROW, CHILI BEAN...
WAAAAAAAAAAAAAH!
HELP!
FLOP!

HMM...

Measure!

IT'S A NEW WORLD RECORD!

YAAAAAAAAY.

Next event: Boxing!

POW!

SOCK!

POW!

BLACK SOYBEAN! YOU'RE SUCH A TOUGH FIGHTER! WHAT'S YOUR SECRET?

THAT'S EASY!

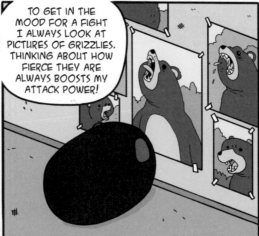

TO GET IN THE MOOD FOR A FIGHT I ALWAYS LOOK AT PICTURES OF GRIZZLIES. THINKING ABOUT HOW FIERCE THEY ARE ALWAYS BOOSTS MY ATTACK POWER!

OH NO! BLACK SOYBEAN'S TRAINING TECHNIQUE IS UNBEATABLE! HOW CAN CHILI BEAN WIN AGAINST SO MUCH POWER?

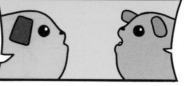

NO PROBLEM. WHAT'S THE ONE ANIMAL EVEN FIERCER THAN A GRIZZLY BEAR?

A REALLY ANGRY HAMSTER?

NO...

A DINOSAUR!

OF COURSE! BRILLIANT!

WE'LL GET CHILI BEAN TO LOOK AT PICTURES OF DINOSAURS!

WITH DINO-POWER ON OUR SIDE, BLACK SOYBEAN WON'T STAND A CHANCE!

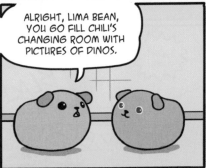

ALRIGHT, LIMA BEAN, YOU GO FILL CHILI'S CHANGING ROOM WITH PICTURES OF DINOS.

AND IT'S VERY IMPORTANT THAT YOU DO EXACTLY WHAT I SAY. DON'T TRY TO CHANGE THE PLAN AT THE LAST MINUTE.

OF COURSE, I WOULD NEVER DO THAT.

5 minutes later...

HOW DID IT GO?

WELL...

...I REALIZED THAT YOUR PLAN WAS TERRIBLE. SO AT THE LAST MINUTE, I DECIDED TO HANG THE DINOSAUR PICTURES IN BLACK SOYBEAN'S ROOM INSTEAD.

MAXPOWER

WOW! THESE PICTURES ARE GREAT! I FEEL FIERCER THAN EVER!

UH-OH...

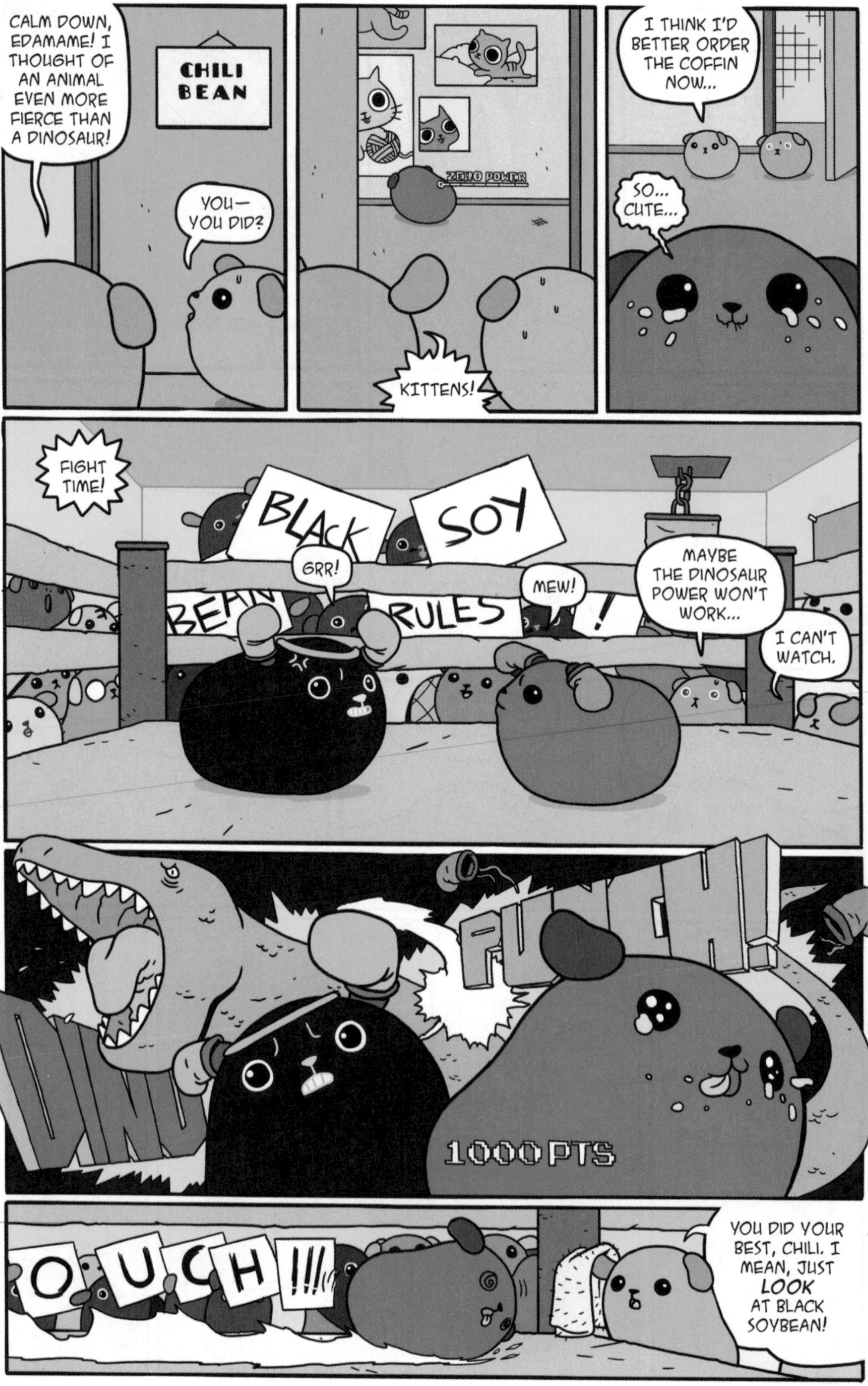
CALM DOWN, EDAMAME! I THOUGHT OF AN ANIMAL EVEN MORE FIERCE THAN A DINOSAUR!
CHILI BEAN
YOU— YOU DID?
ZERO POWER
KITTENS!
I THINK I'D BETTER ORDER THE COFFIN NOW...
SO... CUTE...
FIGHT TIME!
BLACK SOY BEAN RULES !
GRR!
MEW!
MAYBE THE DINOSAUR POWER WON'T WORK...
I CAN'T WATCH.
DINO
PUNCH!
1000 PTS
OUCH!!!
YOU DID YOUR BEST, CHILI. I MEAN, JUST LOOK AT BLACK SOYBEAN!

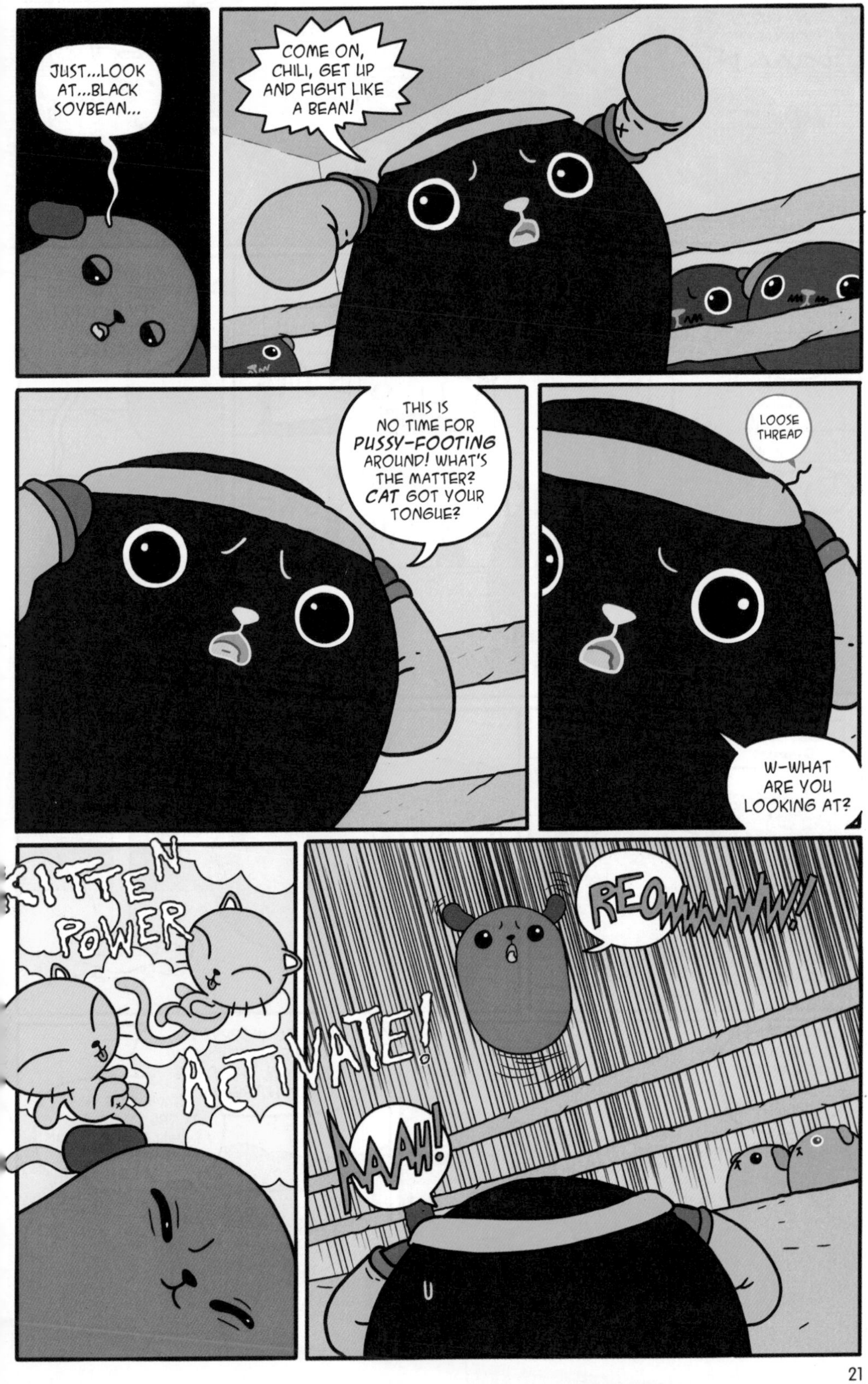
JUST...LOOK AT...BLACK SOYBEAN...
COME ON, CHILI, GET UP AND FIGHT LIKE A BEAN!
THIS IS NO TIME FOR PUSSY-FOOTING AROUND! WHAT'S THE MATTER? CAT GOT YOUR TONGUE?
LOOSE THREAD
W-WHAT ARE YOU LOOKING AT?
KITTEN POWER ACTIVATE!
REOWWWWW!
AAAH!

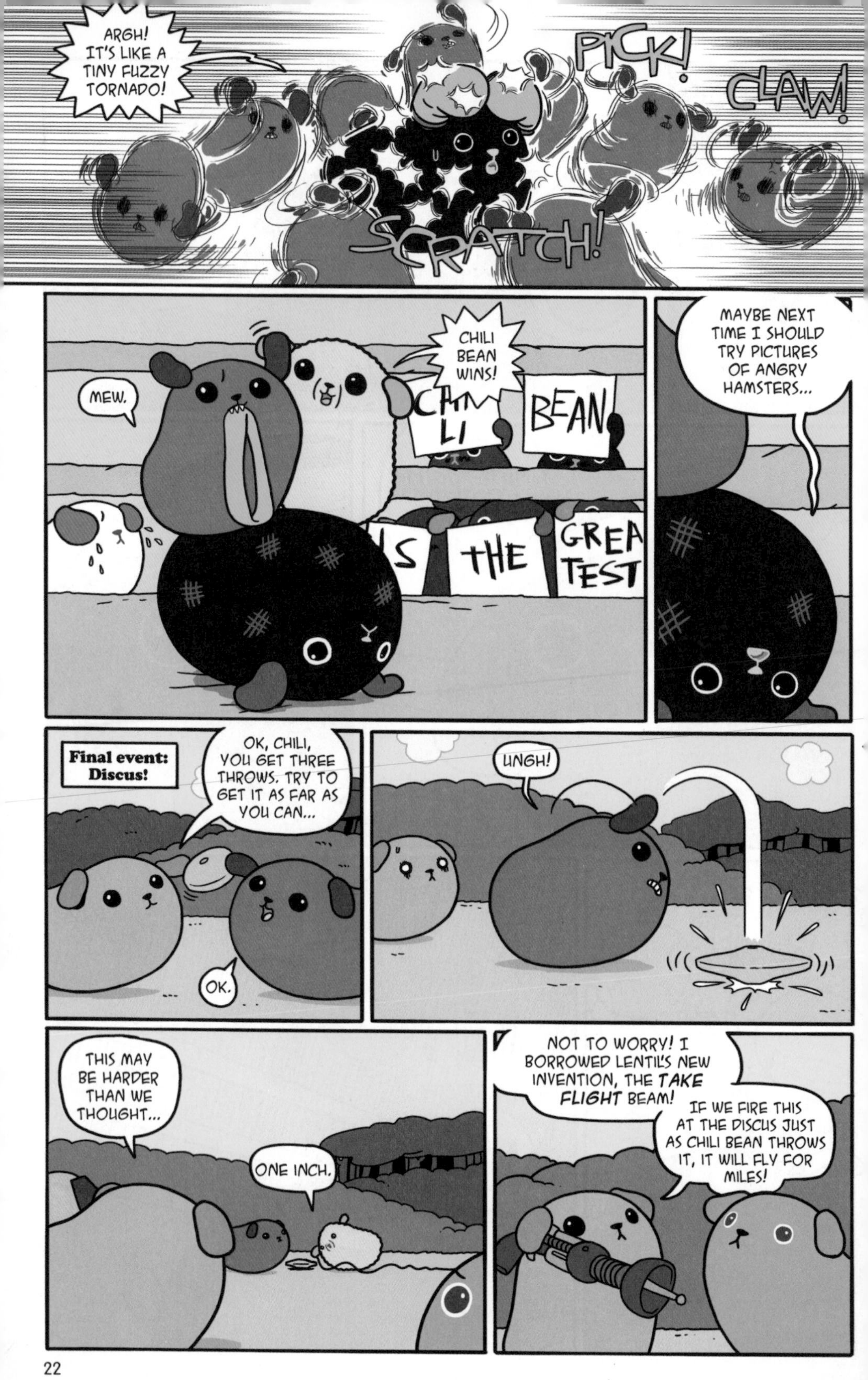
ARGH! IT'S LIKE A TINY FUZZY TORNADO!
PICK!
CLAW!
SCRATCH!
MEW.
CHILI BEAN WINS!
CHI LI BEAN
IS THE GREA TEST
MAYBE NEXT TIME I SHOULD TRY PICTURES OF ANGRY HAMSTERS...
Final event: Discus!
OK, CHILI, YOU GET THREE THROWS. TRY TO GET IT AS FAR AS YOU CAN...
OK.
UNGH!
THIS MAY BE HARDER THAN WE THOUGHT...
ONE INCH.
NOT TO WORRY! I BORROWED LENTIL'S NEW INVENTION, THE TAKE FLIGHT BEAM!
IF WE FIRE THIS AT THE DISCUS JUST AS CHILI BEAN THROWS IT, IT WILL FLY FOR MILES!

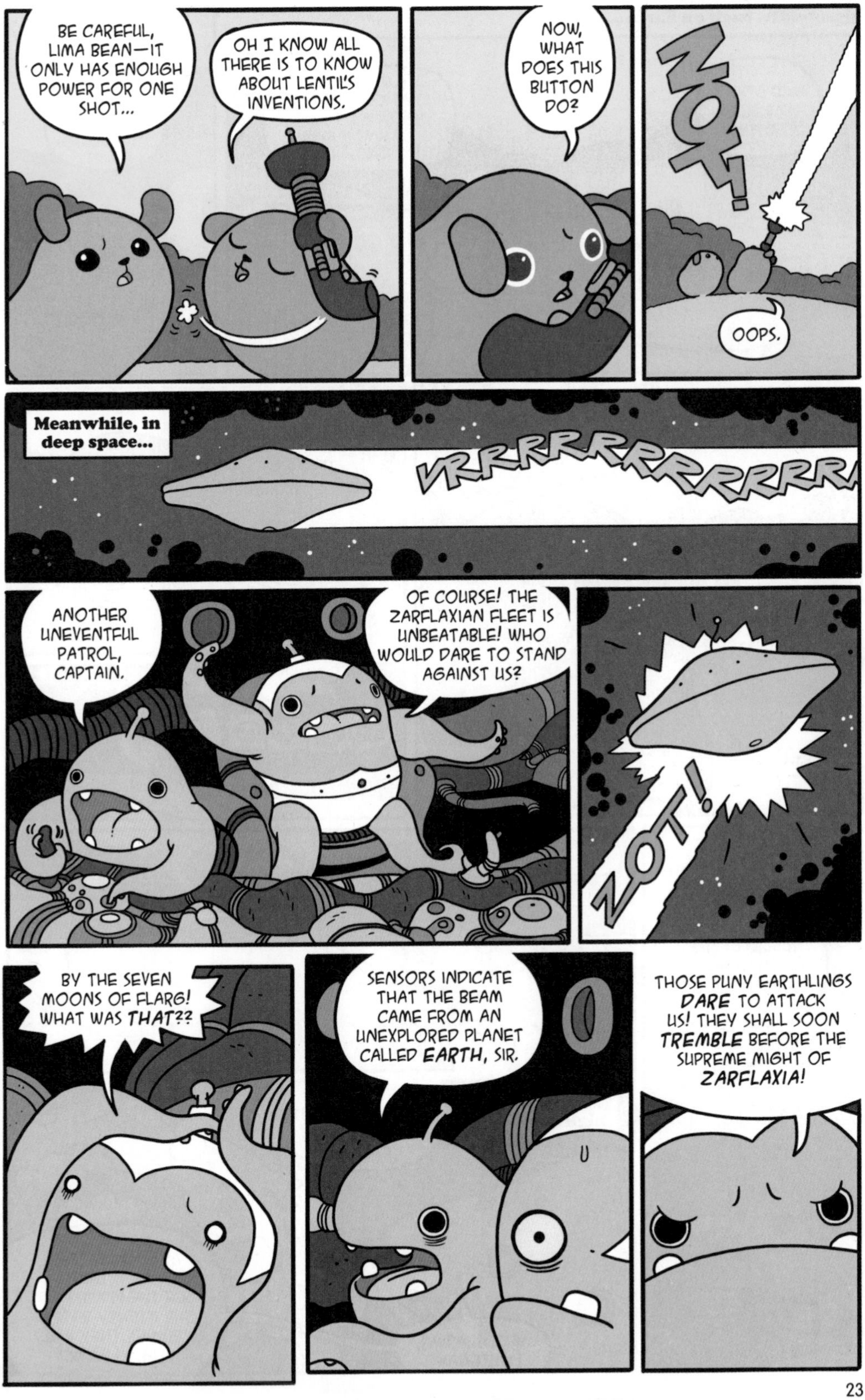
BE CAREFUL, LIMA BEAN—IT ONLY HAS ENOUGH POWER FOR ONE SHOT...
OH I KNOW ALL THERE IS TO KNOW ABOUT LENTIL'S INVENTIONS.
NOW, WHAT DOES THIS BUTTON DO?
WOK!
OOPS.
Meanwhile, in deep space...
VRRRRRRRRRRRR
ANOTHER UNEVENTFUL PATROL, CAPTAIN.
OF COURSE! THE ZARFLAXIAN FLEET IS UNBEATABLE! WHO WOULD DARE TO STAND AGAINST US?
ZOT!
BY THE SEVEN MOONS OF FLARG! WHAT WAS THAT??
SENSORS INDICATE THAT THE BEAM CAME FROM AN UNEXPLORED PLANET CALLED EARTH, SIR.
THOSE PUNY EARTHLINGS DARE TO ATTACK US! THEY SHALL SOON TREMBLE BEFORE THE SUPREME MIGHT OF ZARFLAXIA!

Meanwhile, back on Earth...

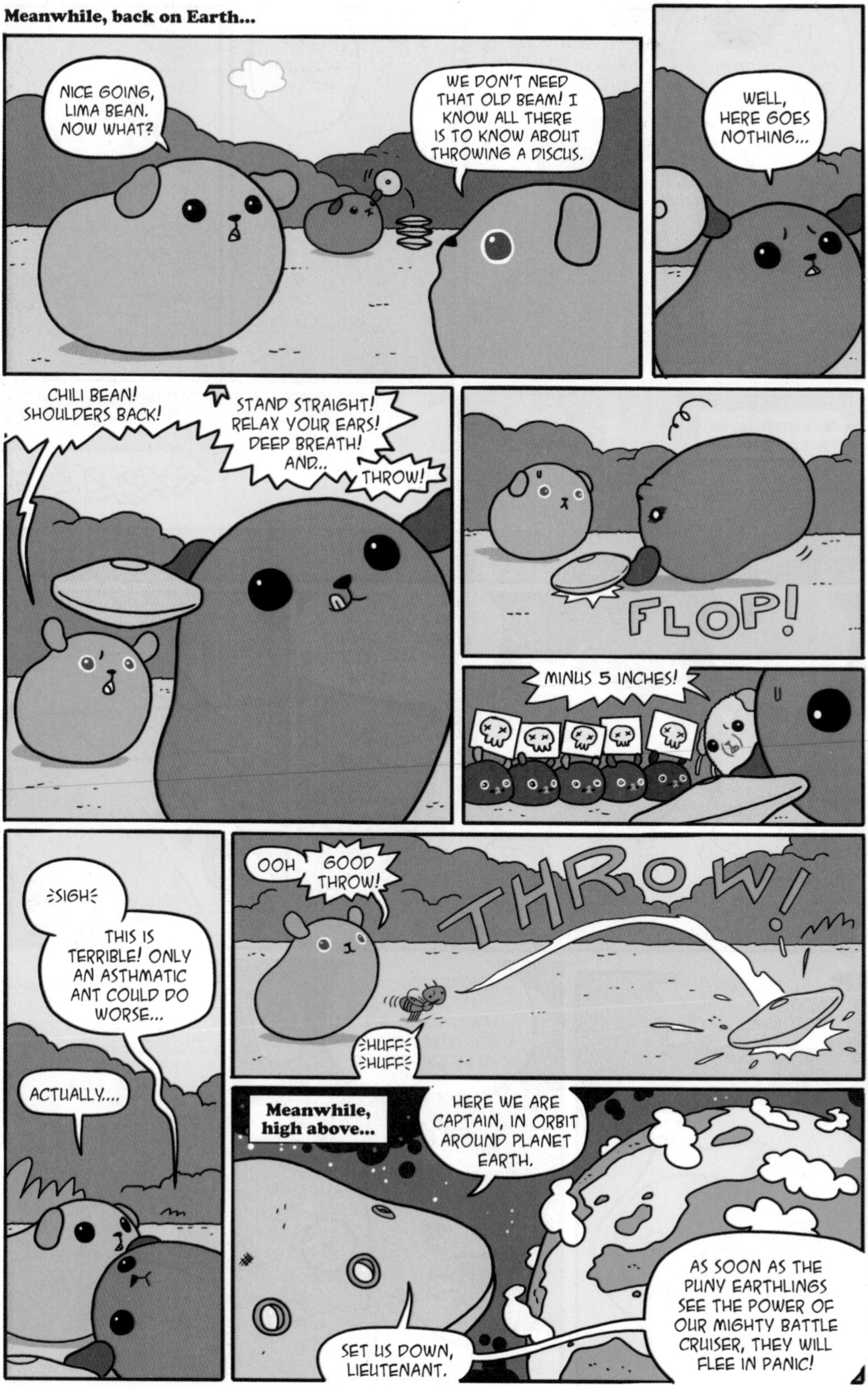
NICE GOING, LIMA BEAN. NOW WHAT?
WE DON'T NEED THAT OLD BEAM! I KNOW ALL THERE IS TO KNOW ABOUT THROWING A DISCUS.
WELL, HERE GOES NOTHING...
CHILI BEAN! SHOULDERS BACK!
STAND STRAIGHT! RELAX YOUR EARS! DEEP BREATH! AND...
THROW!
FLOP!
MINUS 5 INCHES!
SIGH
THIS IS TERRIBLE! ONLY AN ASTHMATIC ANT COULD DO WORSE...
ACTUALLY....
OOH
GOOD THROW!
THROW!
HUFF HUFF
Meanwhile, high above...
HERE WE ARE CAPTAIN, IN ORBIT AROUND PLANET EARTH.
SET US DOWN, LIEUTENANT.
AS SOON AS THE PUNY EARTHLINGS SEE THE POWER OF OUR MIGHTY BATTLE CRUISER, THEY WILL FLEE IN PANIC!

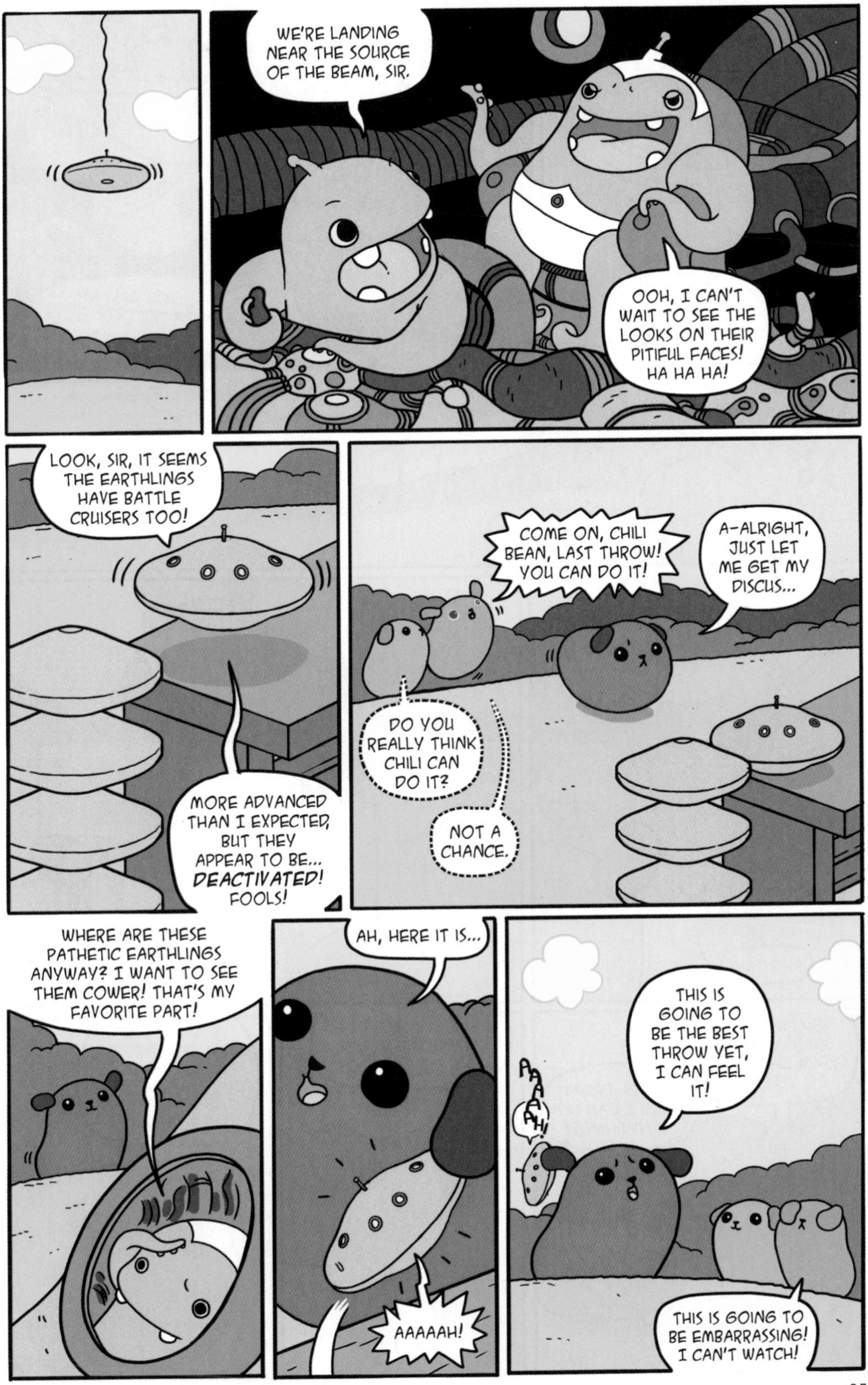
WE'RE LANDING NEAR THE SOURCE OF THE BEAM, SIR.
OOH, I CAN'T WAIT TO SEE THE LOOKS ON THEIR PITIFUL FACES! HA HA HA!
LOOK, SIR, IT SEEMS THE EARTHLINGS HAVE BATTLE CRUISERS TOO!
MORE ADVANCED THAN I EXPECTED, BUT THEY APPEAR TO BE... DEACTIVATED! FOOLS!
COME ON, CHILI BEAN, LAST THROW! YOU CAN DO IT!
A-ALRIGHT, JUST LET ME GET MY DISCUS...
DO YOU REALLY THINK CHILI CAN DO IT?
NOT A CHANCE.
WHERE ARE THESE PATHETIC EARTHLINGS ANYWAY? I WANT TO SEE THEM COWER! THAT'S MY FAVORITE PART!
AH, HERE IT IS...
AAAAAH!
THIS IS GOING TO BE THE BEST THROW YET, I CAN FEEL IT!
THIS IS GOING TO BE EMBARRASSING! I CAN'T WATCH!

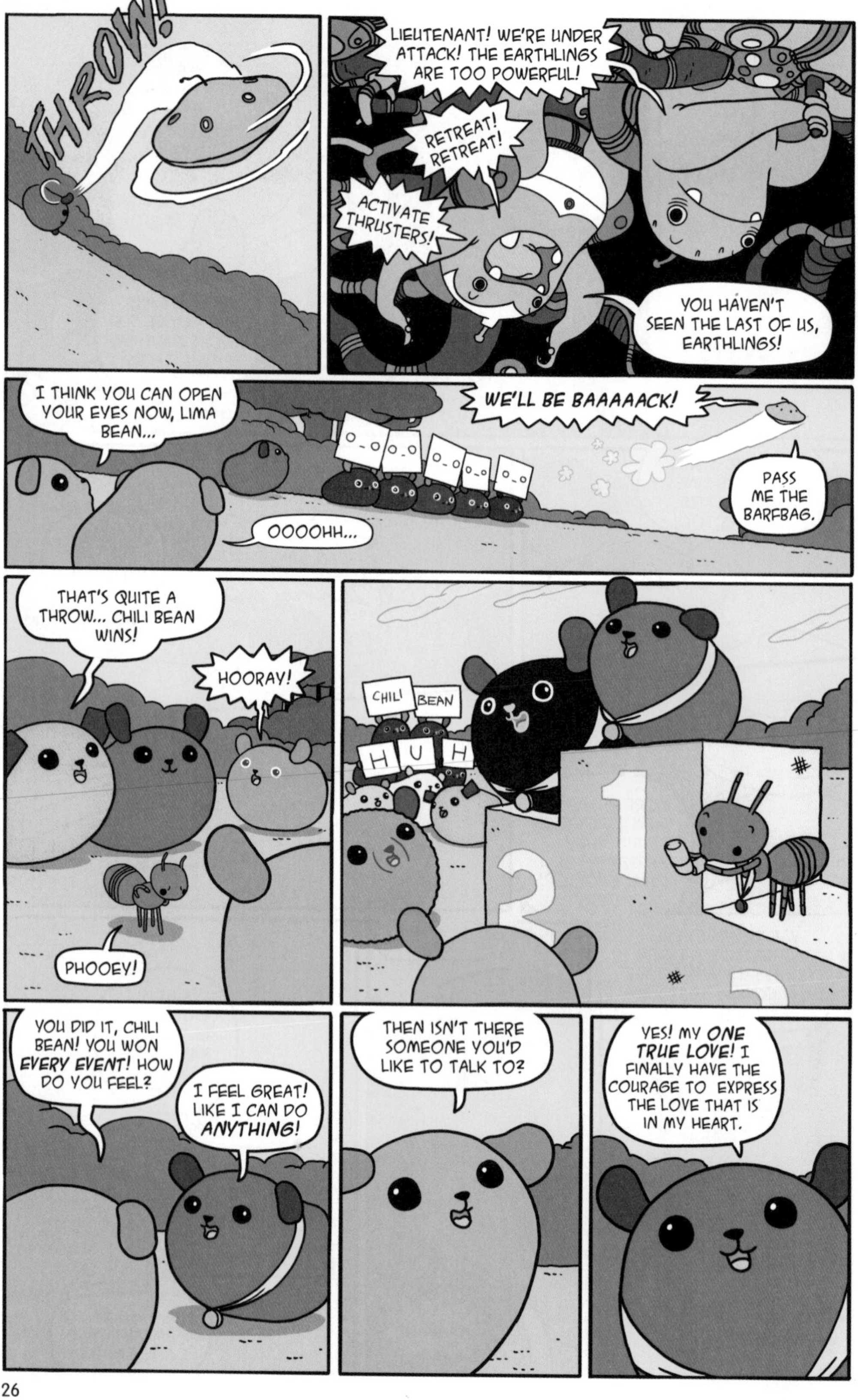
THROW!
LIEUTENANT! WE'RE UNDER ATTACK! THE EARTHLINGS ARE TOO POWERFUL!
RETREAT! RETREAT!
ACTIVATE THRUSTERS!
YOU HAVEN'T SEEN THE LAST OF US, EARTHLINGS!
I THINK YOU CAN OPEN YOUR EYES NOW, LIMA BEAN...
WE'LL BE BAAAAACK!
OOOOHH...
PASS ME THE BARFBAG.
THAT'S QUITE A THROW... CHILI BEAN WINS!
HOORAY!
PHOOEY!
CHILI
BEAN
H U H
1
2
3
YOU DID IT, CHILI BEAN! YOU WON EVERY EVENT! HOW DO YOU FEEL?
I FEEL GREAT! LIKE I CAN DO ANYTHING!
THEN ISN'T THERE SOMEONE YOU'D LIKE TO TALK TO?
YES! MY ONE TRUE LOVE! I FINALLY HAVE THE COURAGE TO EXPRESS THE LOVE THAT IS IN MY HEART.

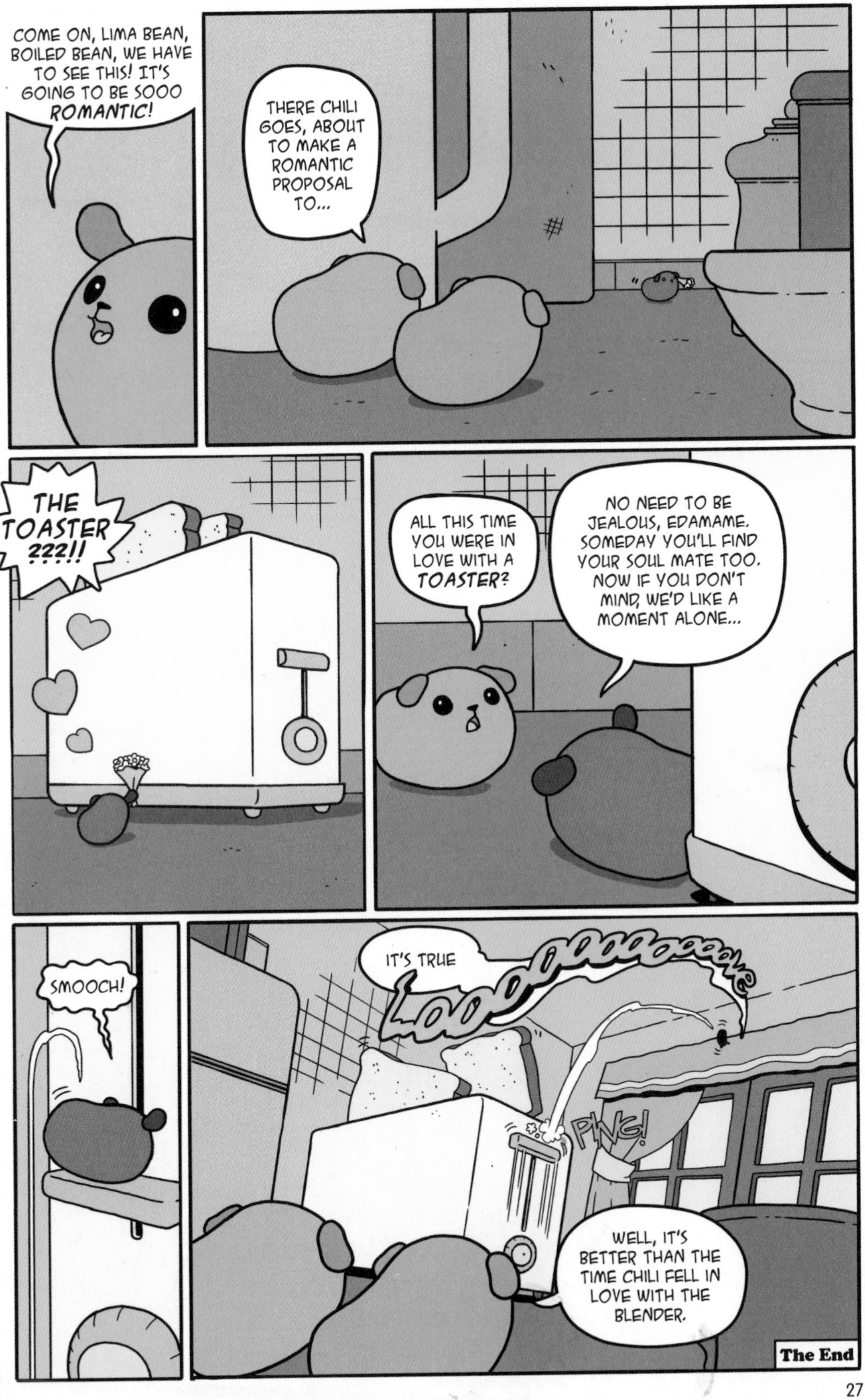
COME ON, LIMA BEAN, BOILED BEAN, WE HAVE TO SEE THIS! IT'S GOING TO BE SOOO ROMANTIC!
THERE CHILI GOES, ABOUT TO MAKE A ROMANTIC PROPOSAL TO...
THE TOASTER ???!!
ALL THIS TIME YOU WERE IN LOVE WITH A TOASTER?
NO NEED TO BE JEALOUS, EDAMAME. SOMEDAY YOU'LL FIND YOUR SOUL MATE TOO. NOW IF YOU DON'T MIND, WE'D LIKE A MOMENT ALONE...
SMOOCH!
IT'S TRUE
LOOOOOOOOOOVE
PING!
WELL, IT'S BETTER THAN THE TIME CHILI FELL IN LOVE WITH THE BLENDER.
The End

mameshiba

We Could Be HEROES!

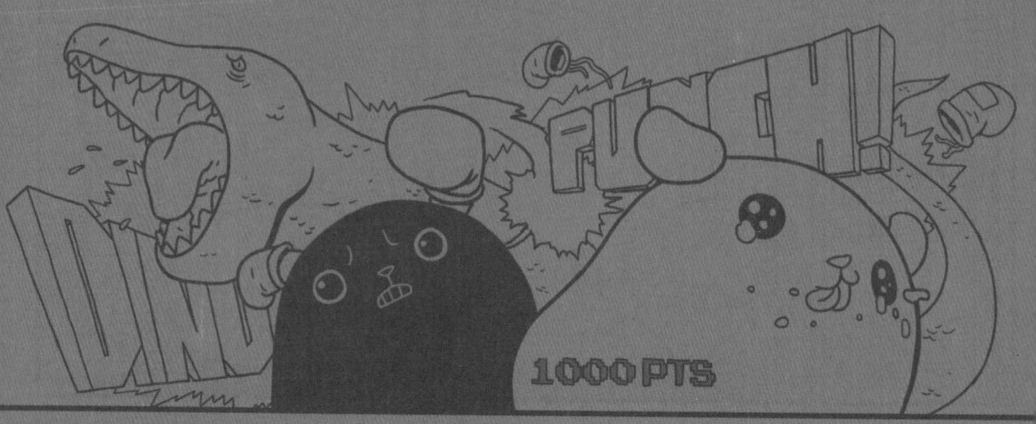
1000 PTS

SWEET TIGER BEAN

STAR-RING Soybean + Tiger Bean

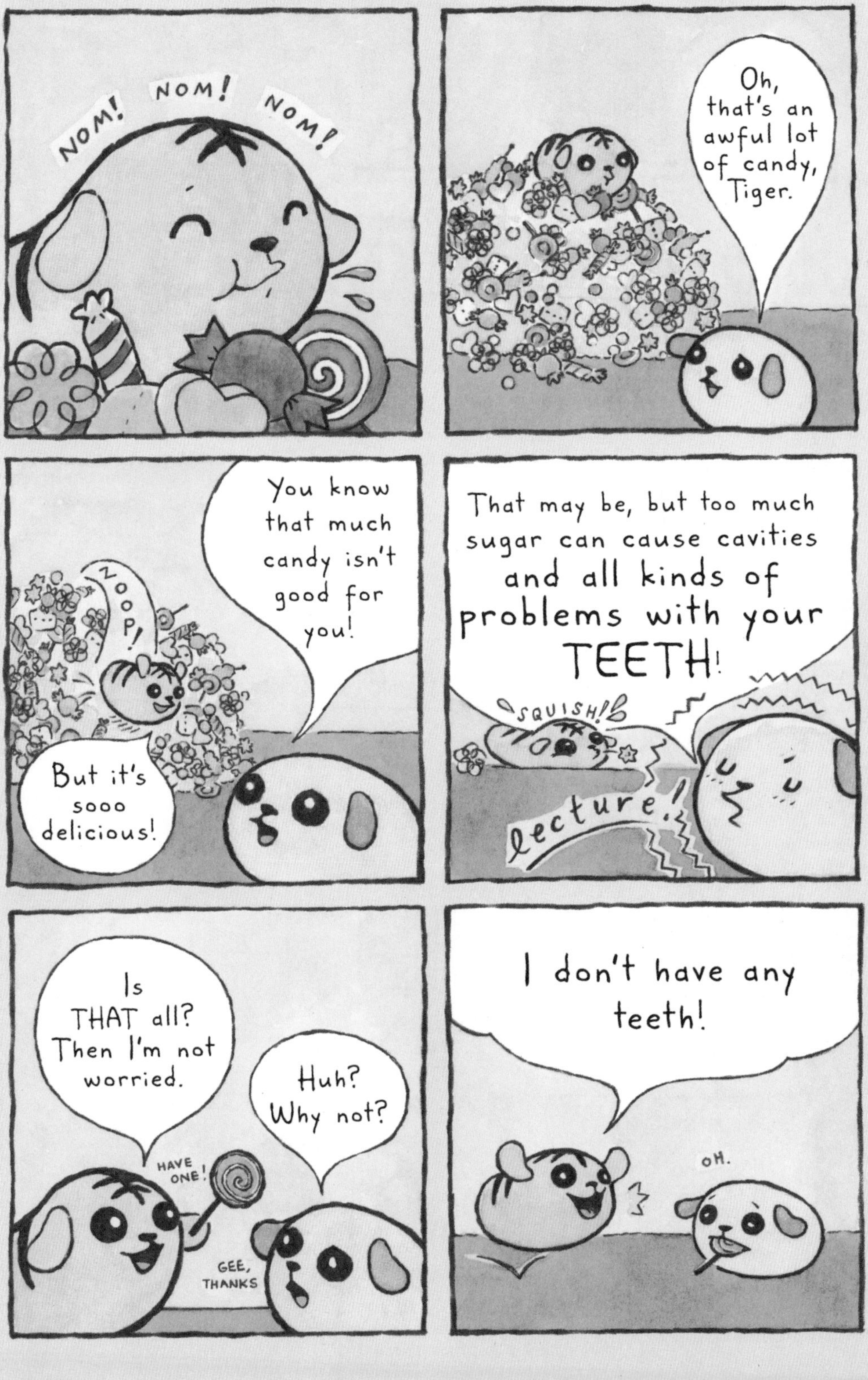
NOM! NOM! NOM!
Oh, that's an awful lot of candy, Tiger.
You know that much candy isn't good for you!
ZOOP!
But it's sooo delicious!
That may be, but too much sugar can cause cavities and all kinds of problems with your TEETH!
SQUISH!
lecture!
Is THAT all? Then I'm not worried.
Huh? Why not?
HAVE ONE!
GEE, THANKS
I don't have any teeth!
OH.

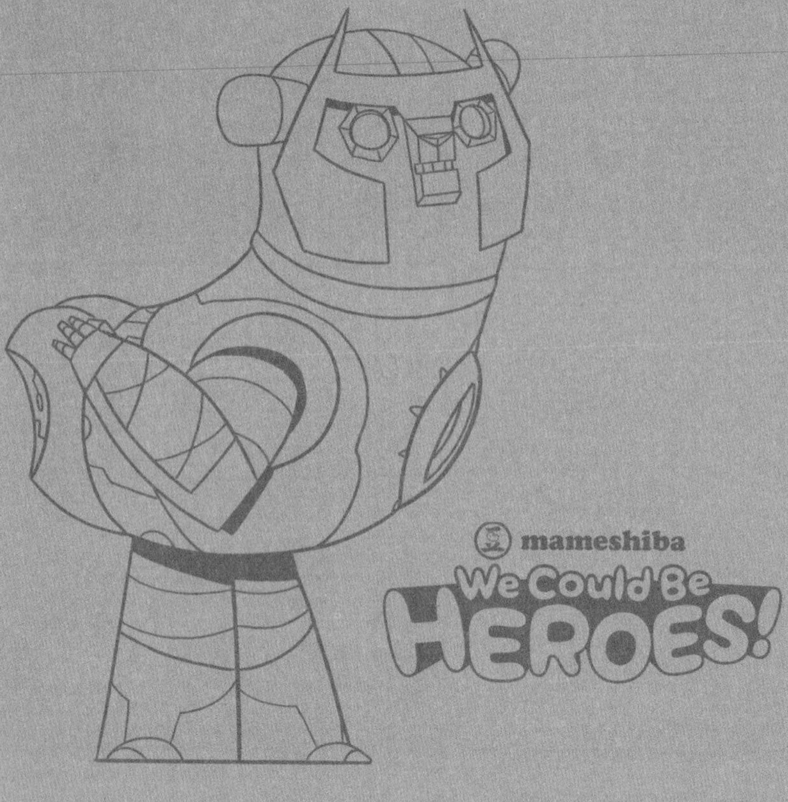

mameshiba

We Could Be HEROES!

A Whole Lotta COCOA

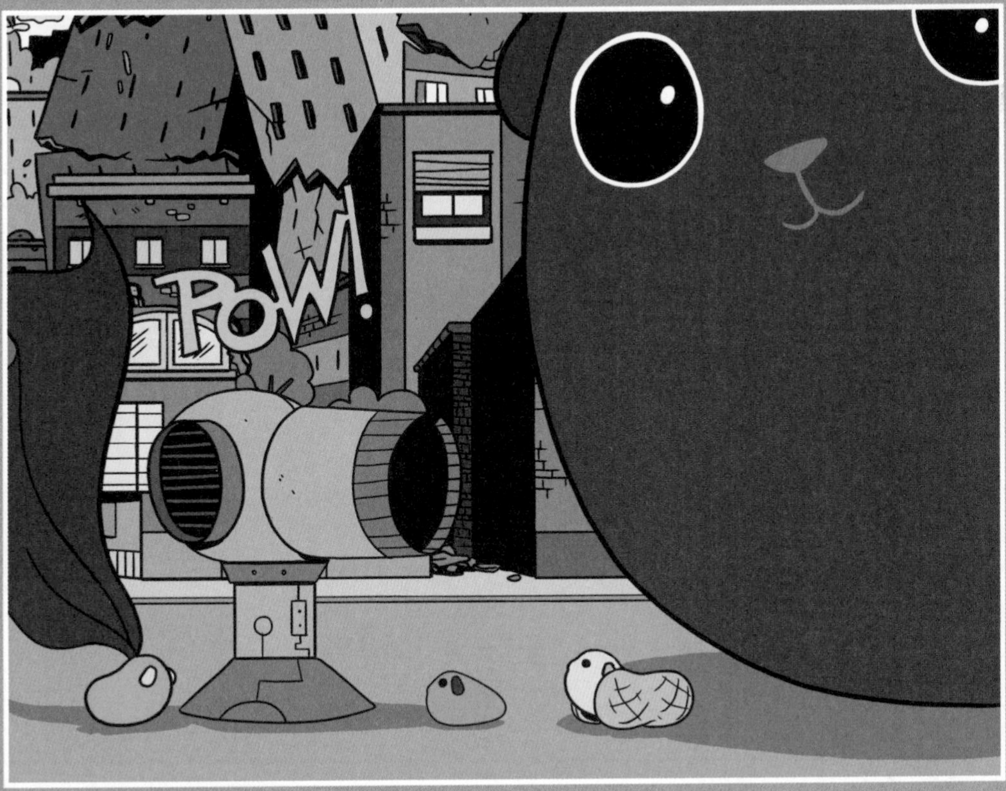
POW!

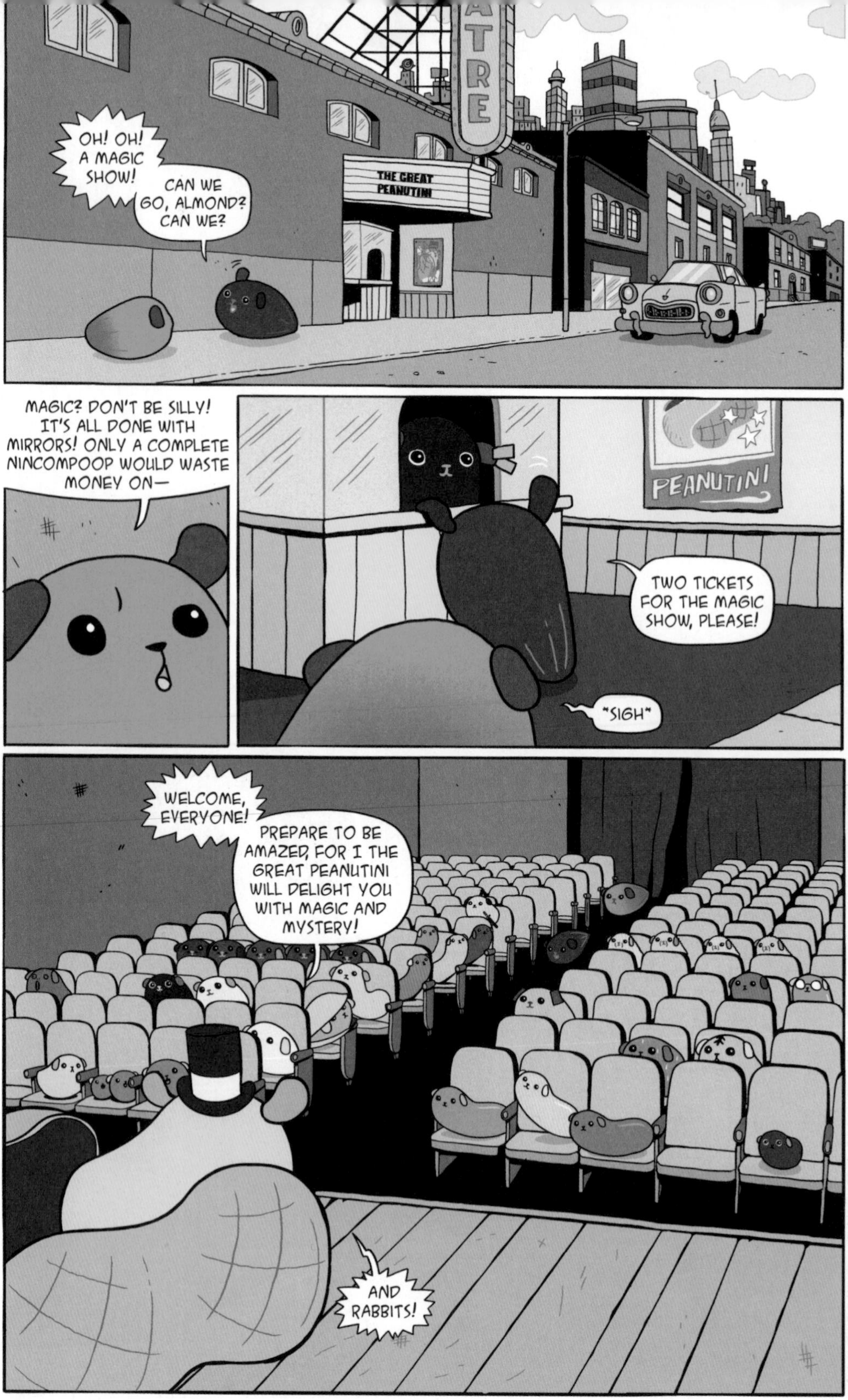
ATRE
THE GREAT PEANUTINI
OH! OH! A MAGIC SHOW!
CAN WE GO, ALMOND? CAN WE?
MAGIC? DON'T BE SILLY! IT'S ALL DONE WITH MIRRORS! ONLY A COMPLETE NINCOMPOOP WOULD WASTE MONEY ON—
PEANUTINI
TWO TICKETS FOR THE MAGIC SHOW, PLEASE!
SIGH
WELCOME, EVERYONE!
PREPARE TO BE AMAZED, FOR I THE GREAT PEANUTINI WILL DELIGHT YOU WITH MAGIC AND MYSTERY!
AND RABBITS!

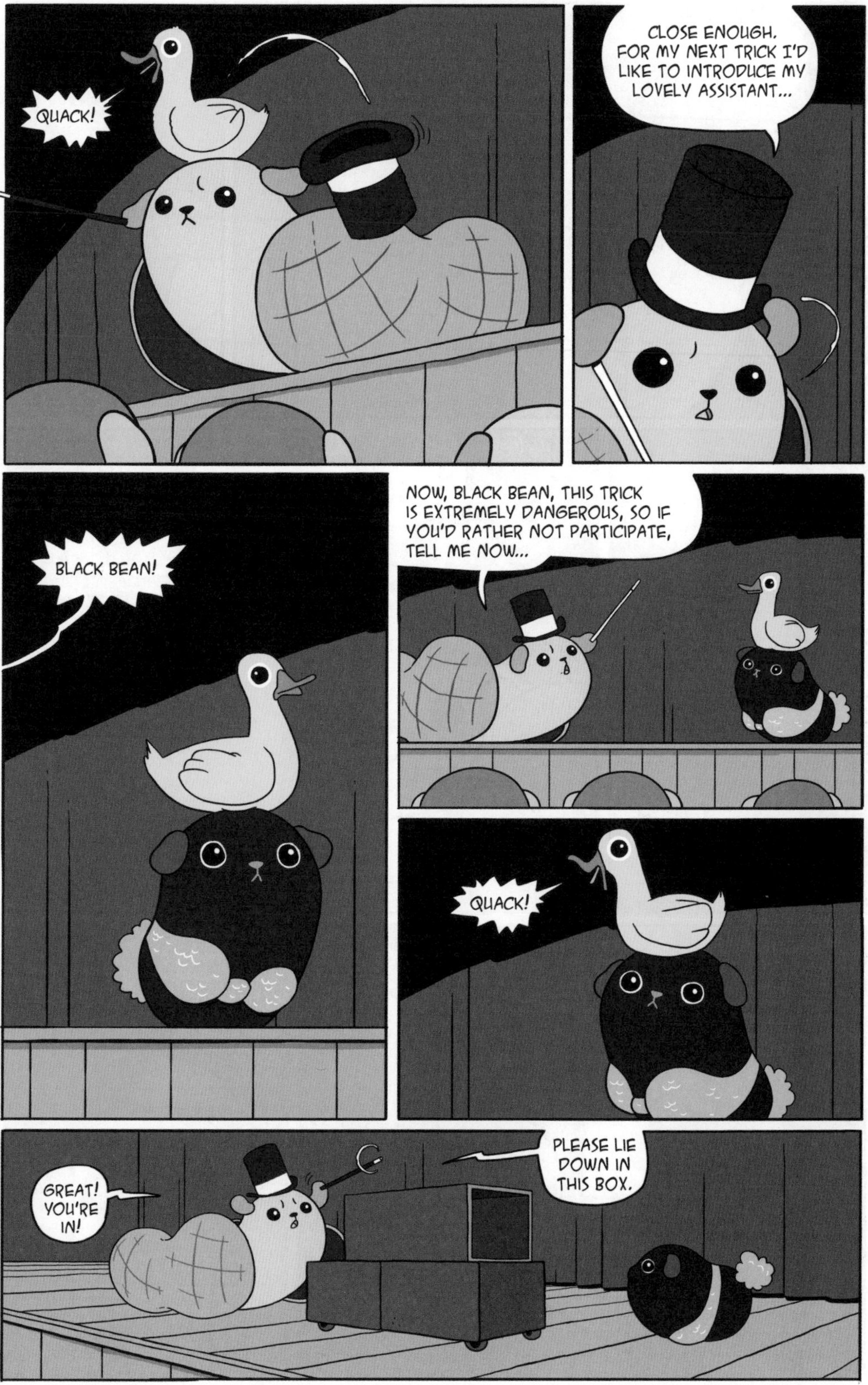
QUACK!
CLOSE ENOUGH. FOR MY NEXT TRICK I'D LIKE TO INTRODUCE MY LOVELY ASSISTANT...
BLACK BEAN!
NOW, BLACK BEAN, THIS TRICK IS EXTREMELY DANGEROUS, SO IF YOU'D RATHER NOT PARTICIPATE, TELL ME NOW...
QUACK!
GREAT! YOU'RE IN!
PLEASE LIE DOWN IN THIS BOX.

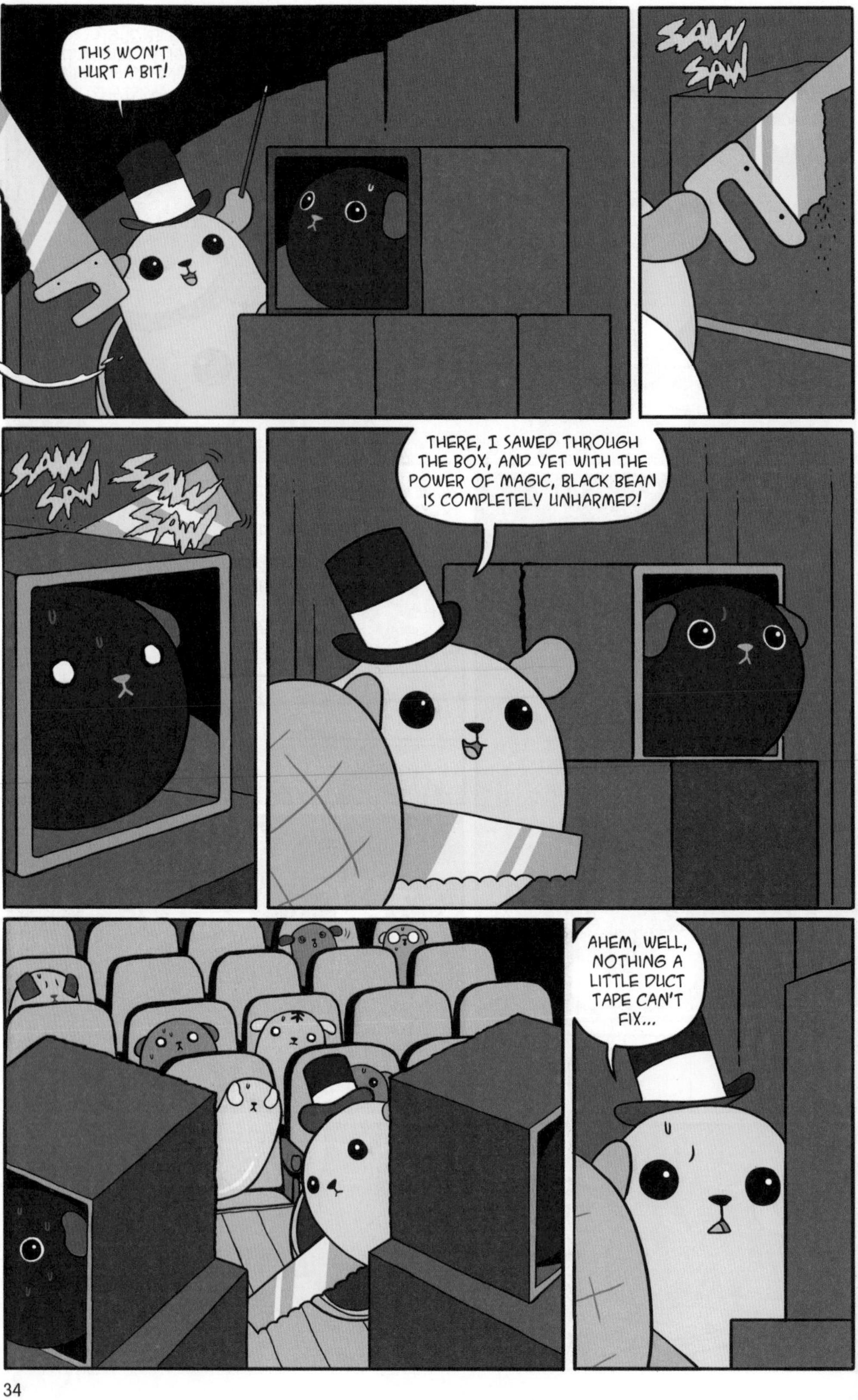
THIS WON'T HURT A BIT!
SAW SAW
SAW SAW SAW SAW
THERE, I SAWED THROUGH THE BOX, AND YET WITH THE POWER OF MAGIC, BLACK BEAN IS COMPLETELY UNHARMED!
AHEM, WELL, NOTHING A LITTLE DUCT TAPE CAN'T FIX...

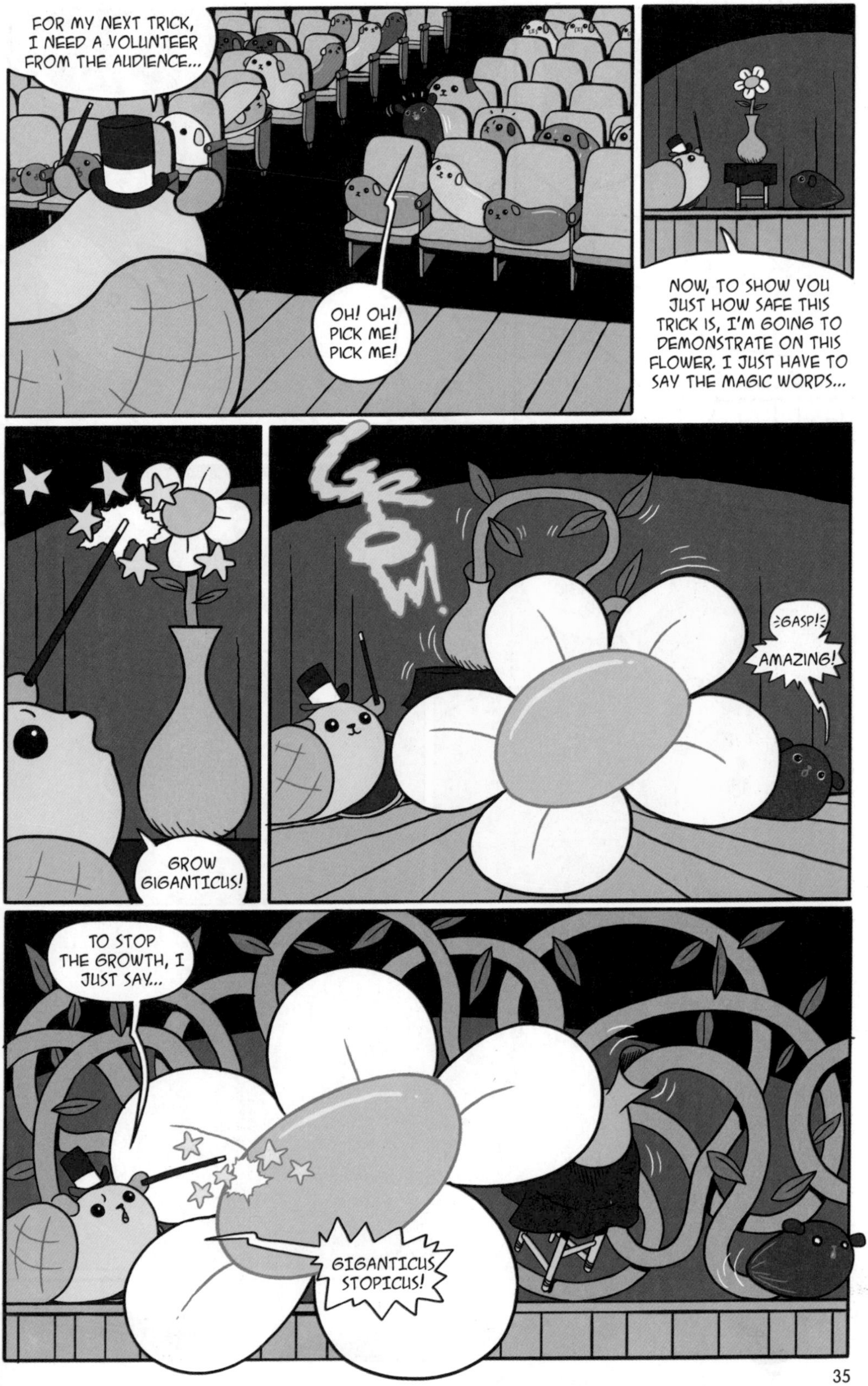
FOR MY NEXT TRICK, I NEED A VOLUNTEER FROM THE AUDIENCE...
OH! OH! PICK ME! PICK ME!
NOW, TO SHOW YOU JUST HOW SAFE THIS TRICK IS, I'M GOING TO DEMONSTRATE ON THIS FLOWER. I JUST HAVE TO SAY THE MAGIC WORDS...
GROW GIGANTICUS!
GROW!
GASP!
AMAZING!
TO STOP THE GROWTH, I JUST SAY...
GIGANTICUS STOPICUS!

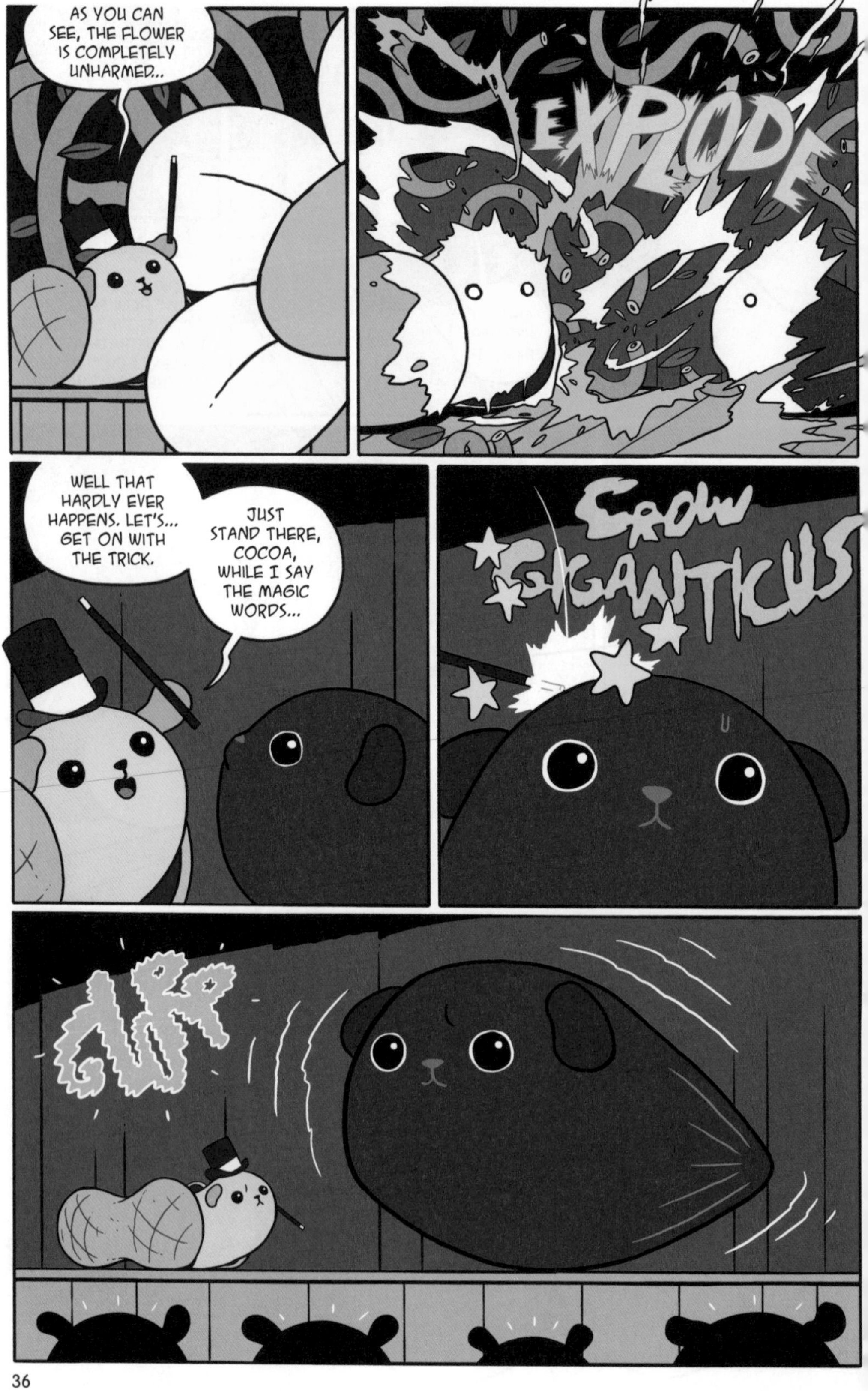
AS YOU CAN SEE, THE FLOWER IS COMPLETELY UNHARMED...
EXPLODE
WELL THAT HARDLY EVER HAPPENS. LET'S... GET ON WITH THE TRICK.
JUST STAND THERE, COCOA, WHILE I SAY THE MAGIC WORDS...
GROW GIGANTICUS
GLIP

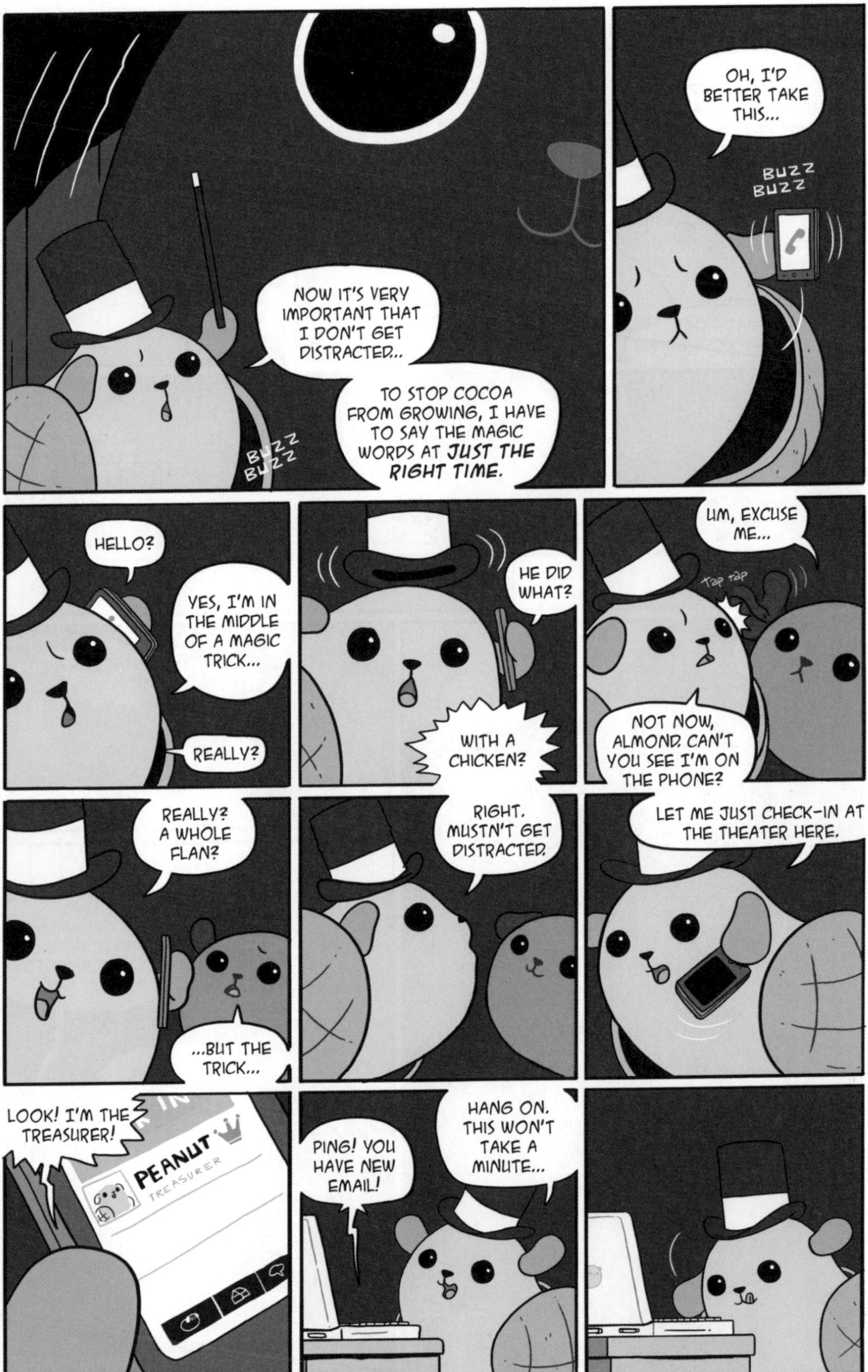
NOW IT'S VERY IMPORTANT THAT I DON'T GET DISTRACTED...
TO STOP COCOA FROM GROWING, I HAVE TO SAY THE MAGIC WORDS AT JUST THE RIGHT TIME.
BUZZ BUZZ
OH, I'D BETTER TAKE THIS...
BUZZ BUZZ
HELLO?
YES, I'M IN THE MIDDLE OF A MAGIC TRICK...
REALLY?
HE DID WHAT?
WITH A CHICKEN?
UM, EXCUSE ME...
TAP TAP
NOT NOW, ALMOND. CAN'T YOU SEE I'M ON THE PHONE?
REALLY? A WHOLE FLAN?
...BUT THE TRICK...
RIGHT. MUSTN'T GET DISTRACTED.
LET ME JUST CHECK-IN AT THE THEATER HERE.
LOOK! I'M THE TREASURER!
PEANUT
TREASURER
PING! YOU HAVE NEW EMAIL!
HANG ON. THIS WON'T TAKE A MINUTE...

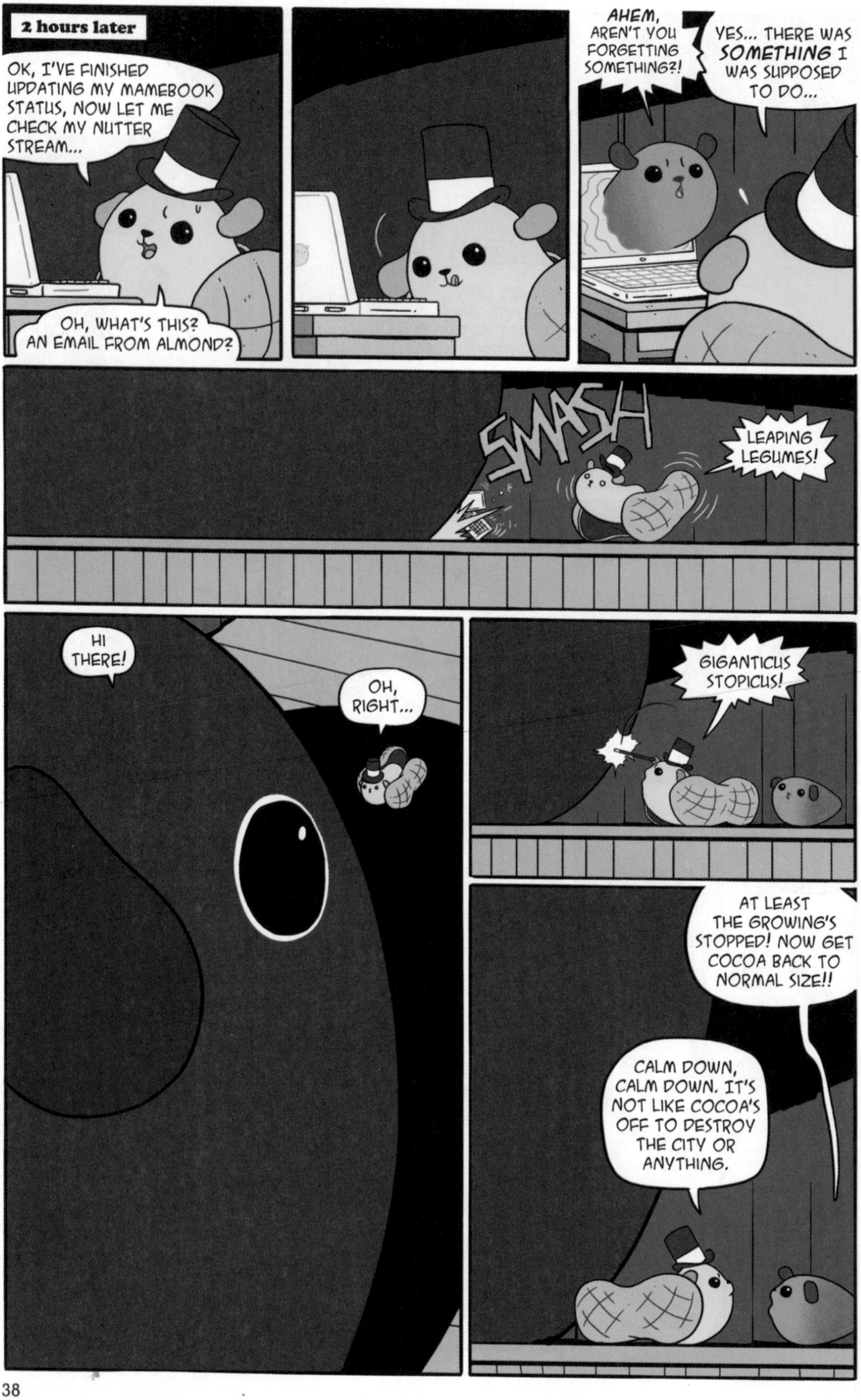
2 hours later
OK, I'VE FINISHED UPDATING MY MAMEBOOK STATUS, NOW LET ME CHECK MY NUTTER STREAM...
OH, WHAT'S THIS? AN EMAIL FROM ALMOND?
AHEM, AREN'T YOU FORGETTING SOMETHING?!
YES... THERE WAS SOMETHING I WAS SUPPOSED TO DO...
SMASH
LEAPING LEGUMES!
HI THERE!
OH, RIGHT...
GIGANTICUS STOPICUS!
AT LEAST THE GROWING'S STOPPED! NOW GET COCOA BACK TO NORMAL SIZE!!
CALM DOWN, CALM DOWN. IT'S NOT LIKE COCOA'S OFF TO DESTROY THE CITY OR ANYTHING.

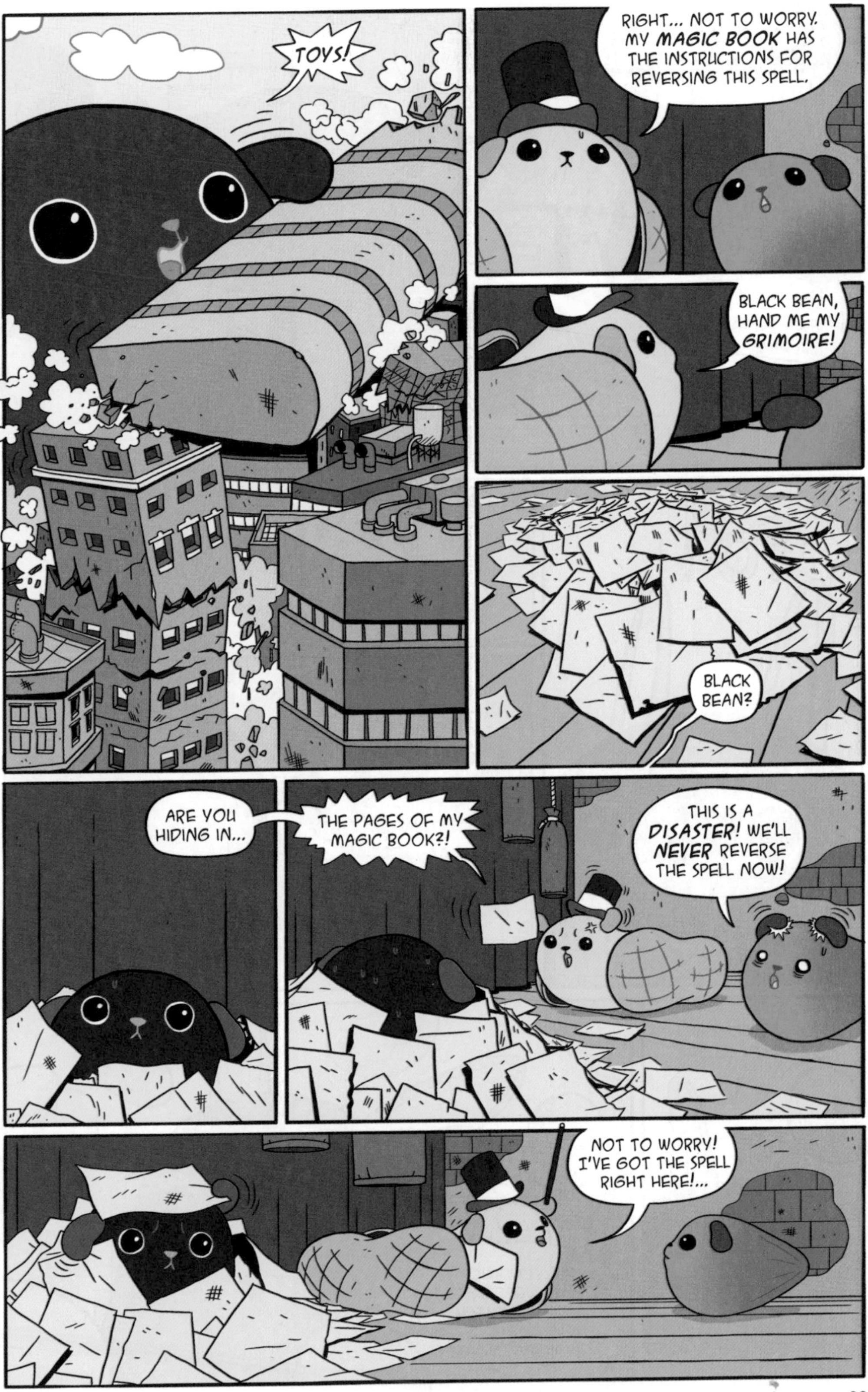
TOYS!
RIGHT... NOT TO WORRY. MY MAGIC BOOK HAS THE INSTRUCTIONS FOR REVERSING THIS SPELL.
BLACK BEAN, HAND ME MY GRIMOIRE!
BLACK BEAN?
ARE YOU HIDING IN...
THE PAGES OF MY MAGIC BOOK?!
THIS IS A DISASTER! WE'LL NEVER REVERSE THE SPELL NOW!
NOT TO WORRY! I'VE GOT THE SPELL RIGHT HERE!...

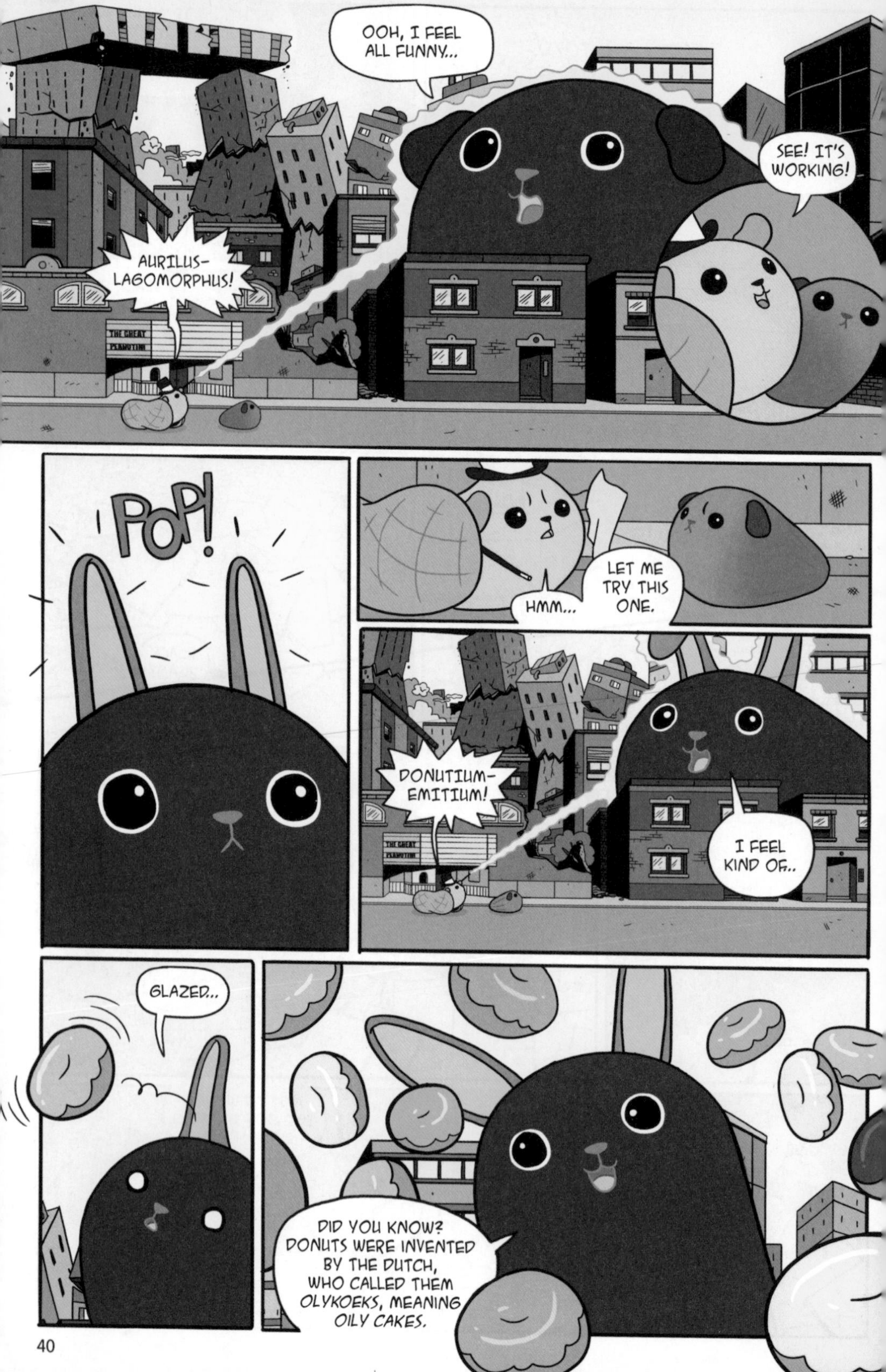
AURILUS-LAGOMORPHUS!
OOH, I FEEL ALL FUNNY...
SEE! IT'S WORKING!
POP!
HMM...
LET ME TRY THIS ONE.
DONUTIUM-EMITIUM!
I FEEL KIND OF...
GLAZED...
DID YOU KNOW? DONUTS WERE INVENTED BY THE DUTCH, WHO CALLED THEM OLYKOEKS, MEANING OILY CAKES.

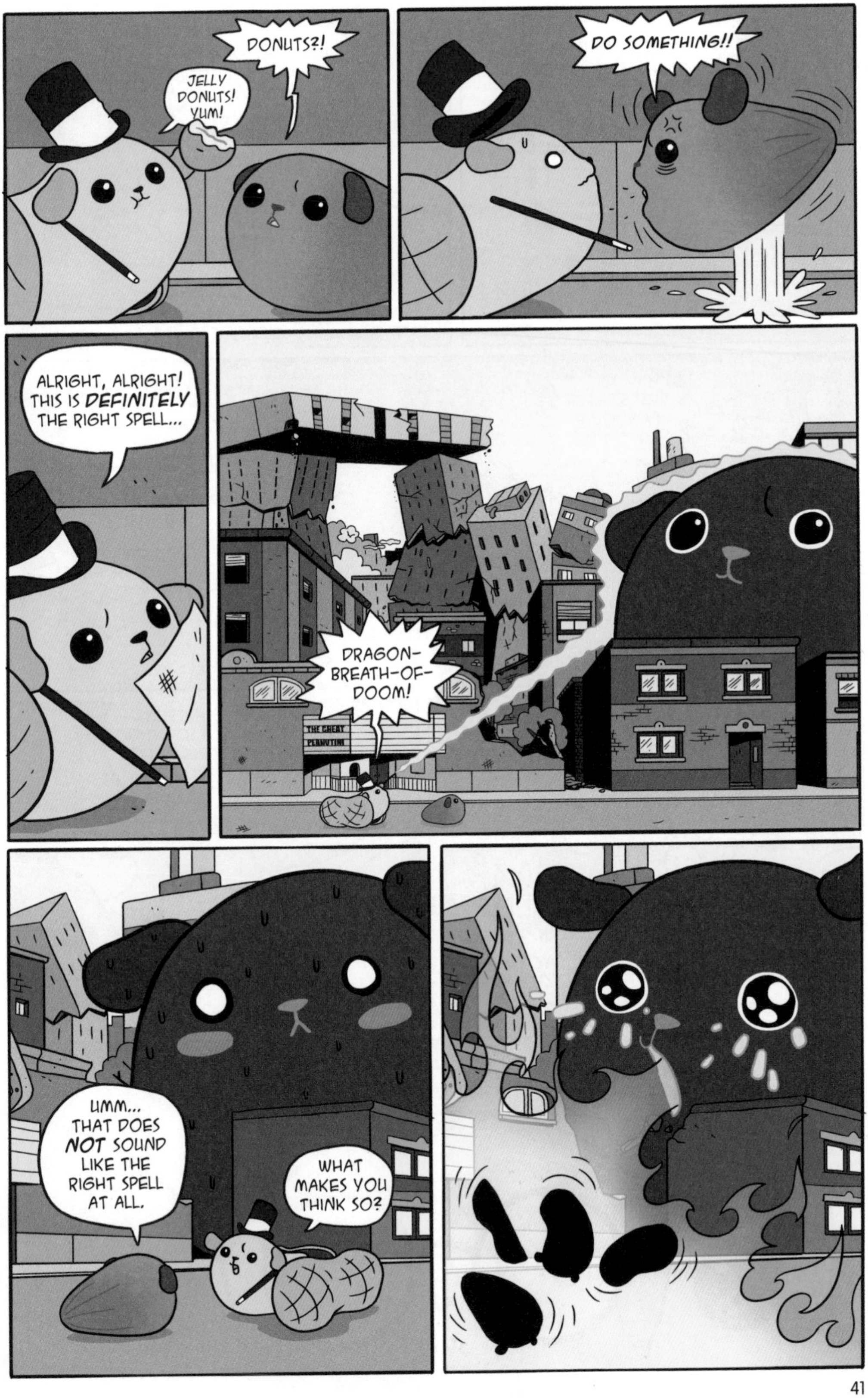
JELLY DONUTS! YUM!
DONUTS?!
DO SOMETHING!!
ALRIGHT, ALRIGHT! THIS IS DEFINITELY THE RIGHT SPELL...
DRAGON-BREATH-OF-DOOM!
THE GREAT PEANUTINI
UMM... THAT DOES NOT SOUND LIKE THE RIGHT SPELL AT ALL.
WHAT MAKES YOU THINK SO?

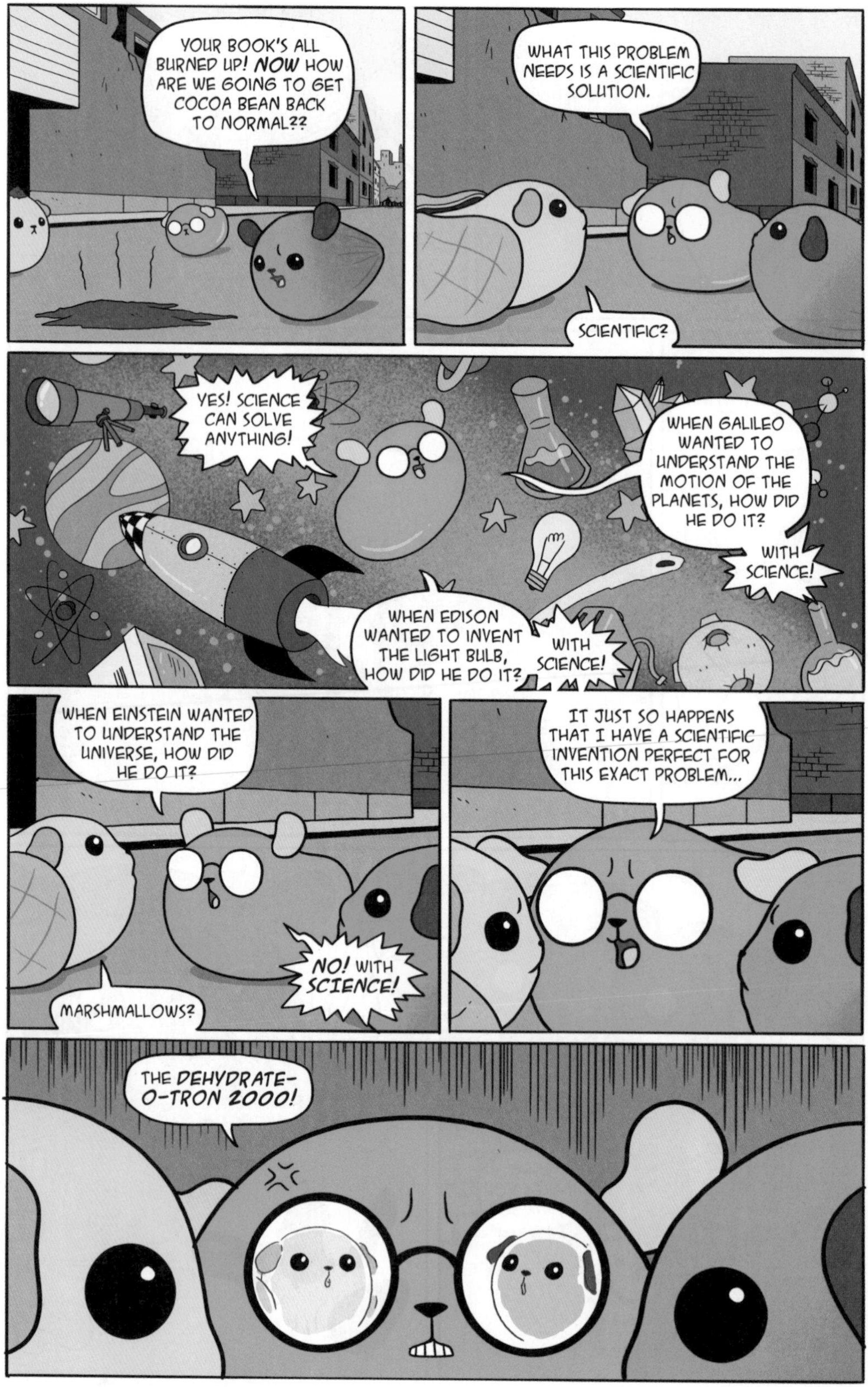
YOUR BOOK'S ALL BURNED UP! NOW HOW ARE WE GOING TO GET COCOA BEAN BACK TO NORMAL??
WHAT THIS PROBLEM NEEDS IS A SCIENTIFIC SOLUTION.
SCIENTIFIC?
YES! SCIENCE CAN SOLVE ANYTHING!
WHEN GALILEO WANTED TO UNDERSTAND THE MOTION OF THE PLANETS, HOW DID HE DO IT?
WITH SCIENCE!
WHEN EDISON WANTED TO INVENT THE LIGHT BULB, HOW DID HE DO IT?
WITH SCIENCE!
WHEN EINSTEIN WANTED TO UNDERSTAND THE UNIVERSE, HOW DID HE DO IT?
MARSHMALLOWS?
NO! WITH SCIENCE!
IT JUST SO HAPPENS THAT I HAVE A SCIENTIFIC INVENTION PERFECT FOR THIS EXACT PROBLEM...
THE DEHYDRATE-O-TRON 2000!

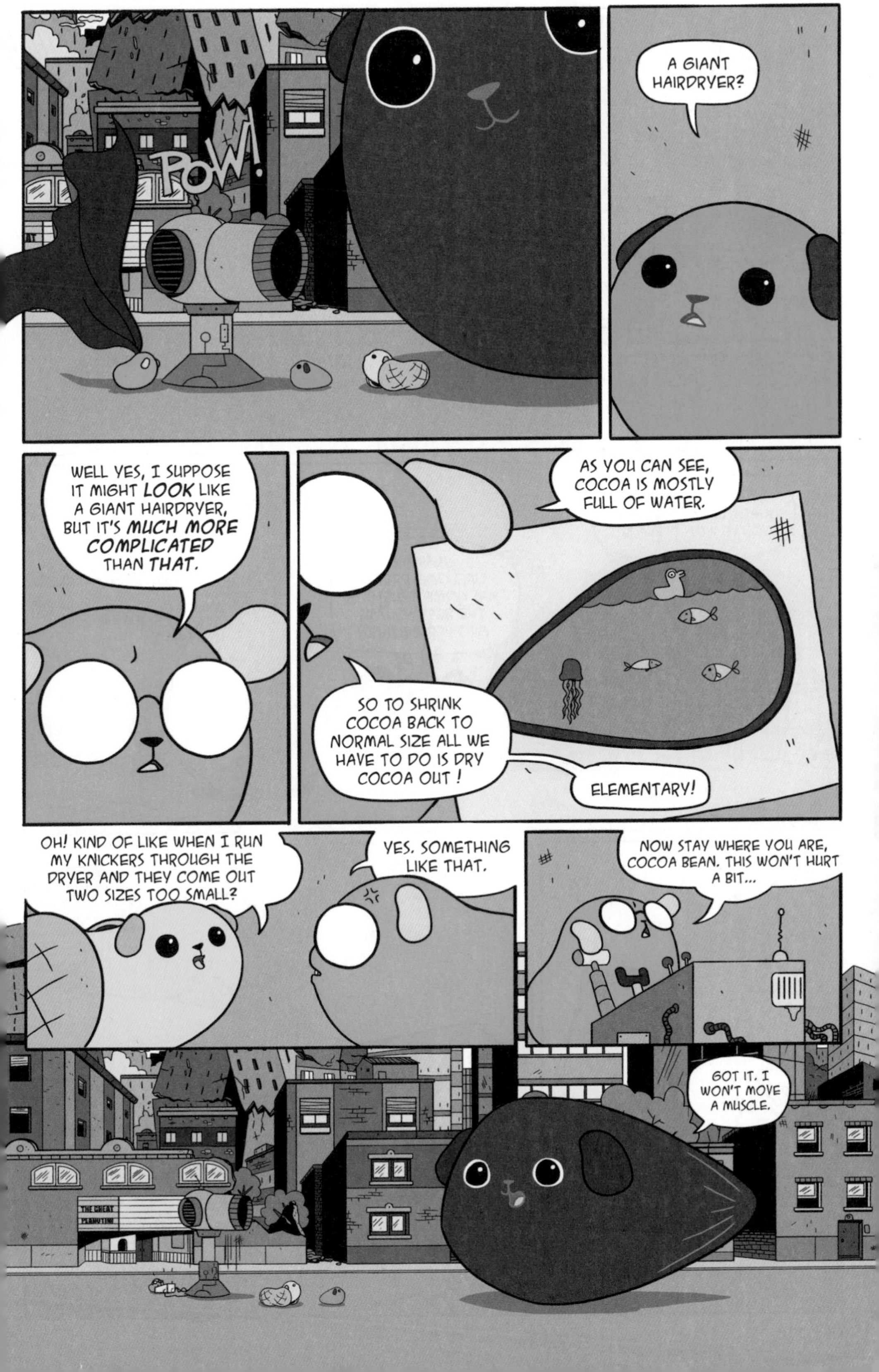
POW!
A GIANT HAIRDRYER?
WELL YES, I SUPPOSE IT MIGHT LOOK LIKE A GIANT HAIRDRYER, BUT IT'S MUCH MORE COMPLICATED THAN THAT.
AS YOU CAN SEE, COCOA IS MOSTLY FULL OF WATER.
SO TO SHRINK COCOA BACK TO NORMAL SIZE ALL WE HAVE TO DO IS DRY COCOA OUT !
ELEMENTARY!
OH! KIND OF LIKE WHEN I RUN MY KNICKERS THROUGH THE DRYER AND THEY COME OUT TWO SIZES TOO SMALL?
YES. SOMETHING LIKE THAT.
NOW STAY WHERE YOU ARE, COCOA BEAN. THIS WON'T HURT A BIT...
GOT IT. I WON'T MOVE A MUSCLE.
THE GREAT PEANUTINI

ACTIVATING DEHYDRATE-O-TRON!
OOH! A TOY CAR!
WHOOOOOOSH!!!
WHAT A MAGNIFICENT SQUASH, CRANBERRY BEAN! YOU'VE WON 1ST PLACE!
YES! MY LIFELONG DREAM HAS COME TRUE! I'M THE BEST SQUASH GROWER AROUND!
COUNTRY FAIR
Shrivel!!

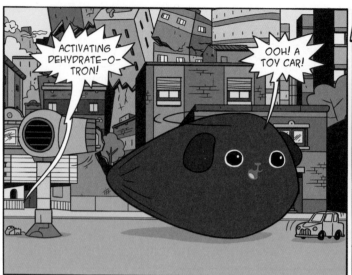

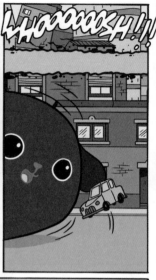

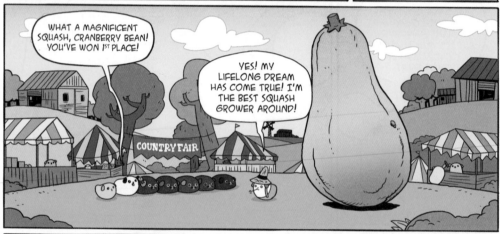

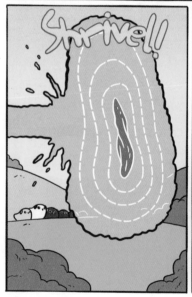

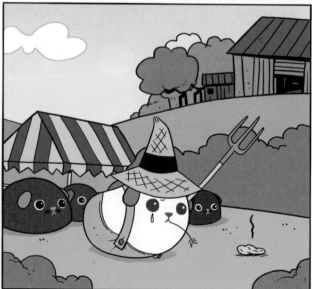

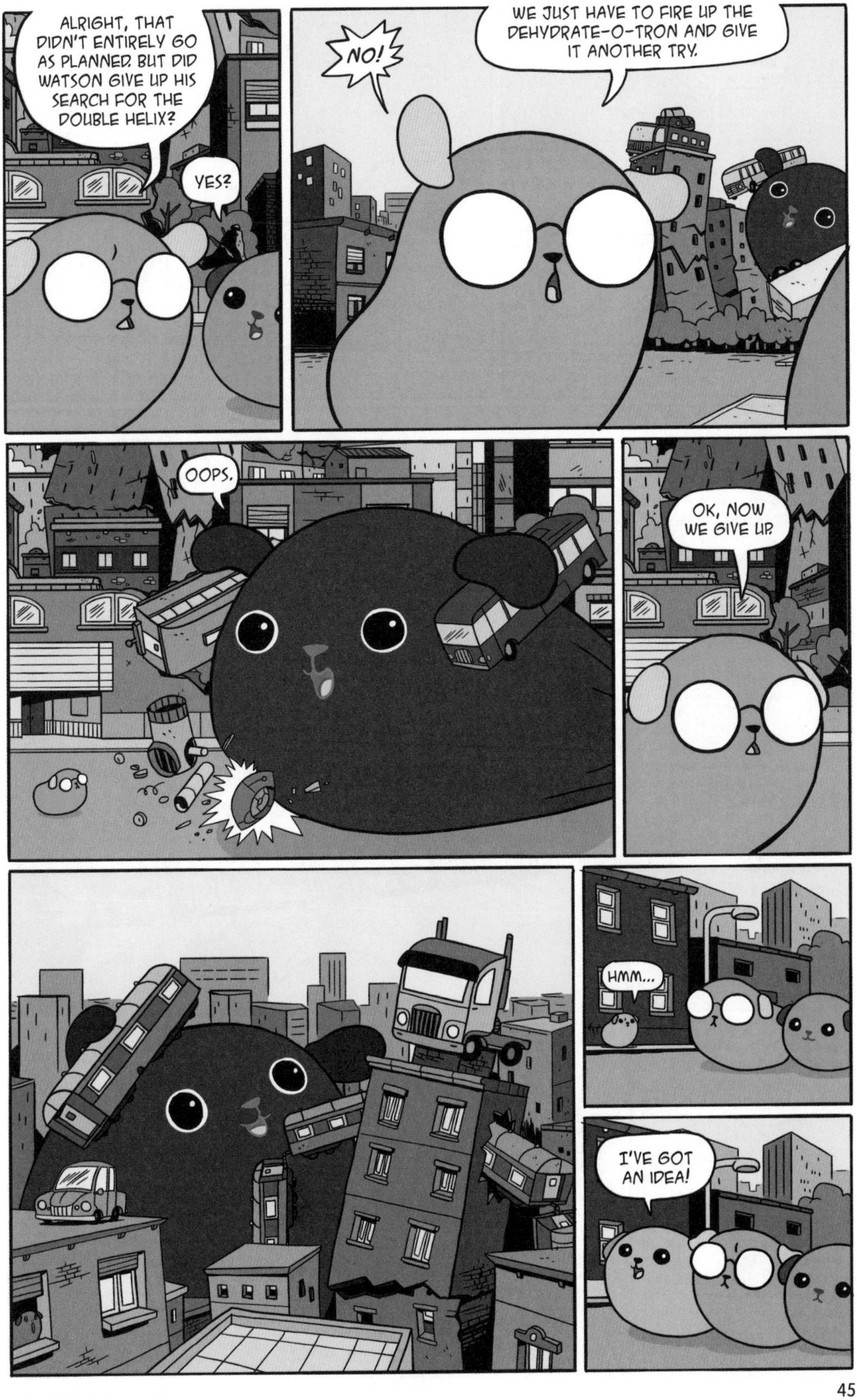
ALRIGHT, THAT DIDN'T ENTIRELY GO AS PLANNED. BUT DID WATSON GIVE UP HIS SEARCH FOR THE DOUBLE HELIX?
YES?
NO!
WE JUST HAVE TO FIRE UP THE DEHYDRATE-O-TRON AND GIVE IT ANOTHER TRY.
OOPS.
OK, NOW WE GIVE UP.
HMM...
I'VE GOT AN IDEA!

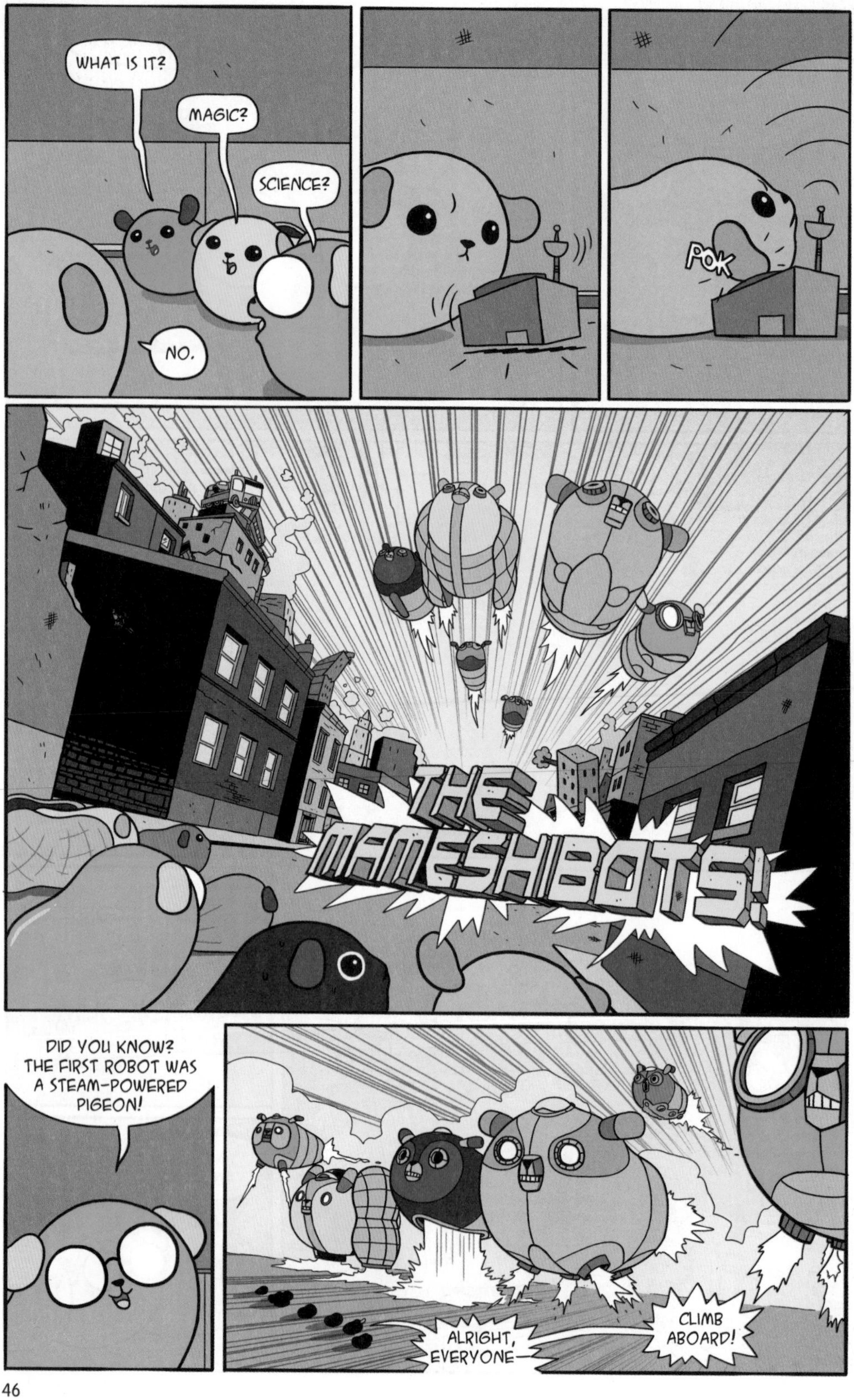
WHAT IS IT?
MAGIC?
SCIENCE?
NO.
POK
THE MAMESHIBOTS!
DID YOU KNOW? THE FIRST ROBOT WAS A STEAM-POWERED PIGEON!
ALRIGHT, EVERYONE—
CLIMB ABOARD!

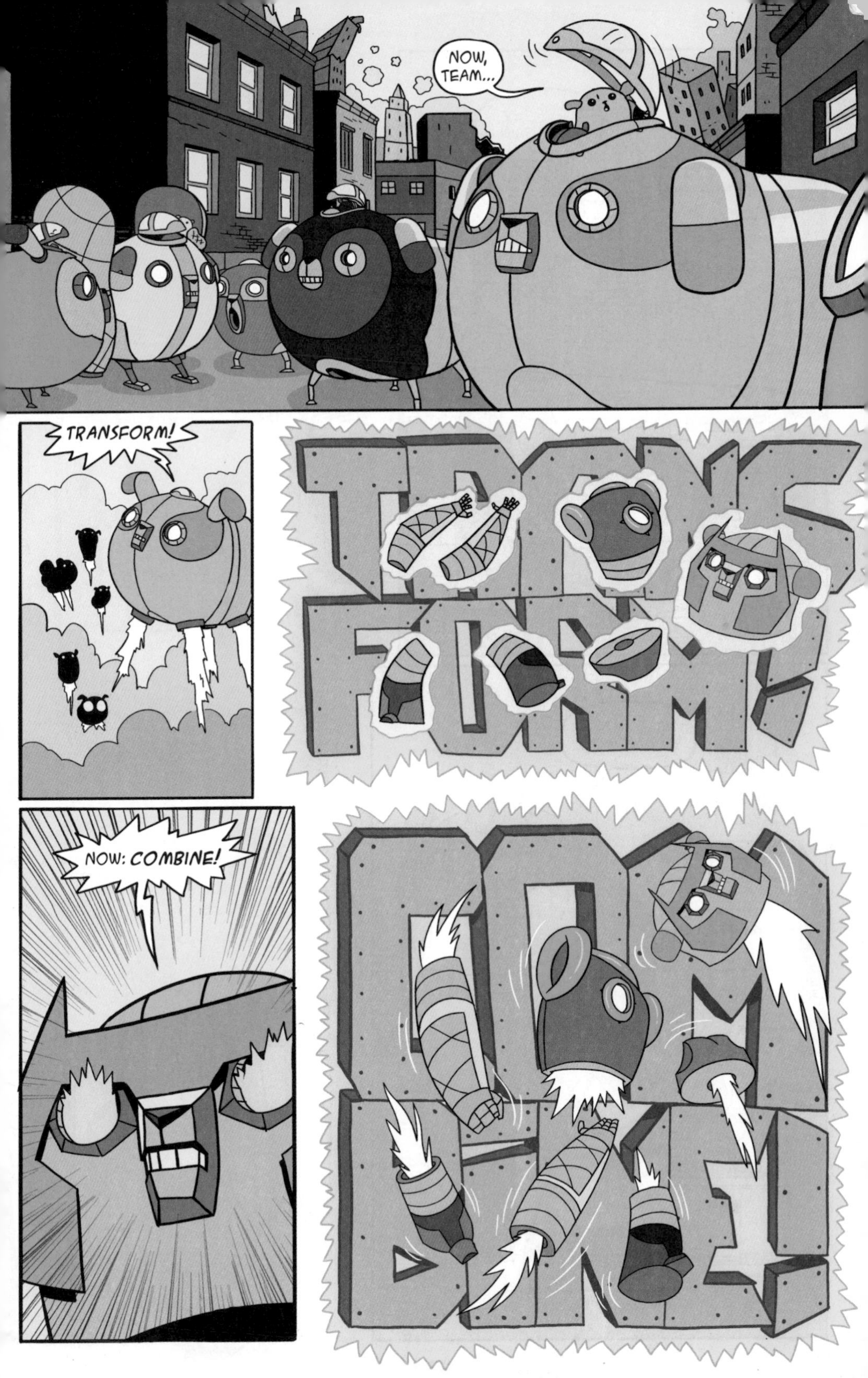
NOW, TEAM...
TRANSFORM!
TRANSFORM!
NOW: COMBINE!
COMBINE!

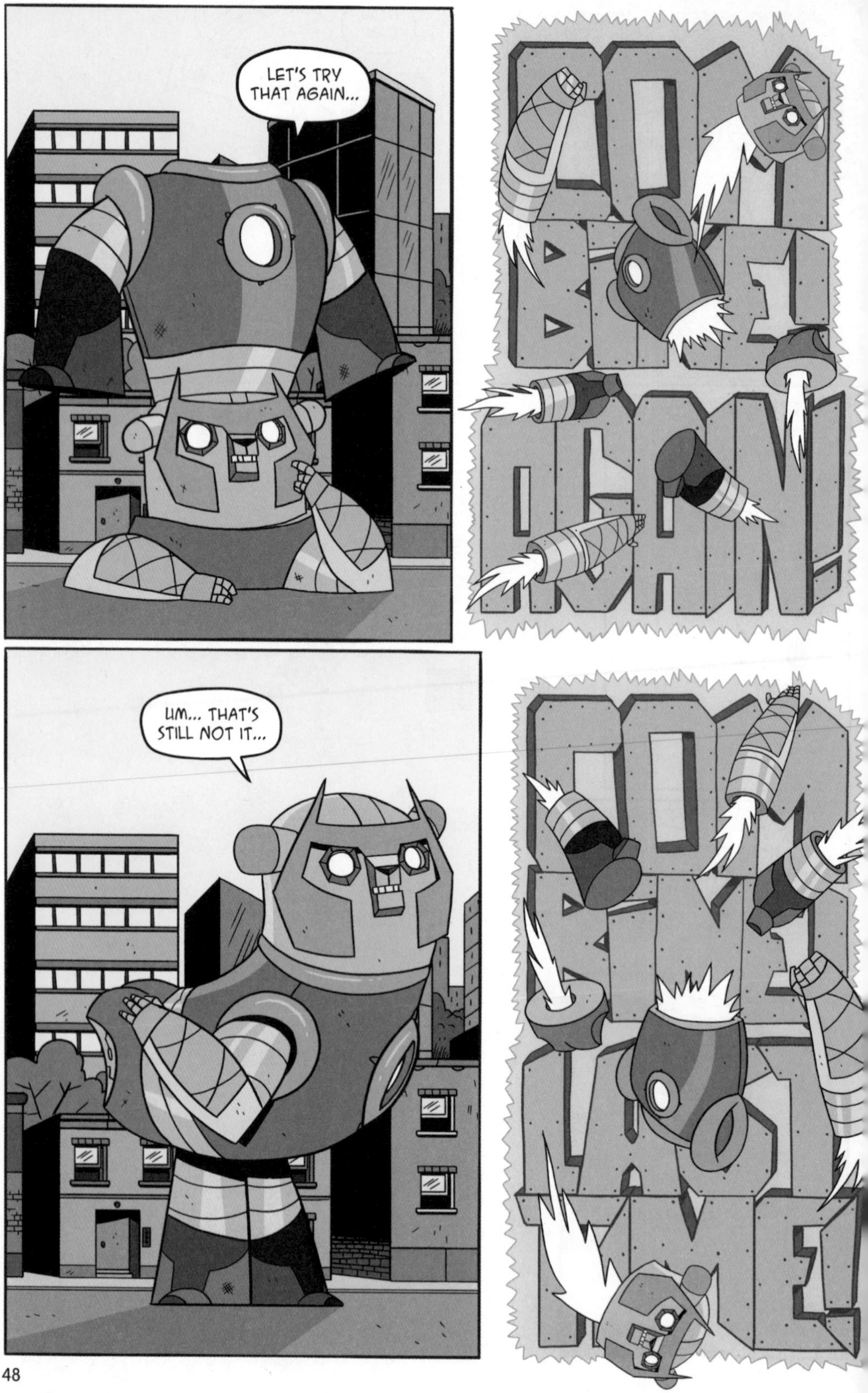
LET'S TRY THAT AGAIN...
UM... THAT'S STILL NOT IT...

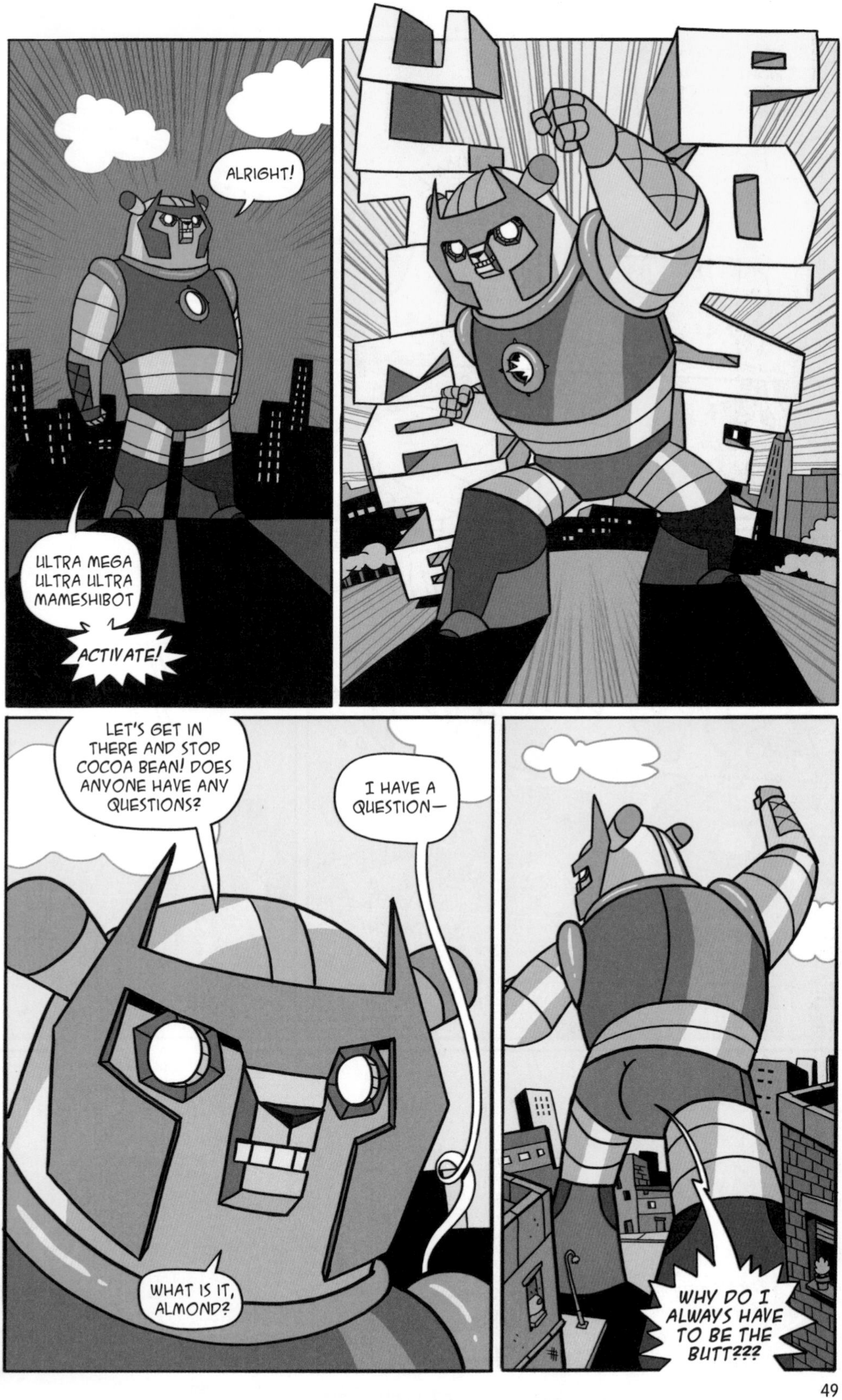
ALRIGHT!
ULTRA MEGA ULTRA ULTRA MAMESHIBOT
ACTIVATE!
LET'S GET IN THERE AND STOP COCOA BEAN! DOES ANYONE HAVE ANY QUESTIONS?
I HAVE A QUESTION—
WHAT IS IT, ALMOND?
WHY DO I ALWAYS HAVE TO BE THE BUTT???

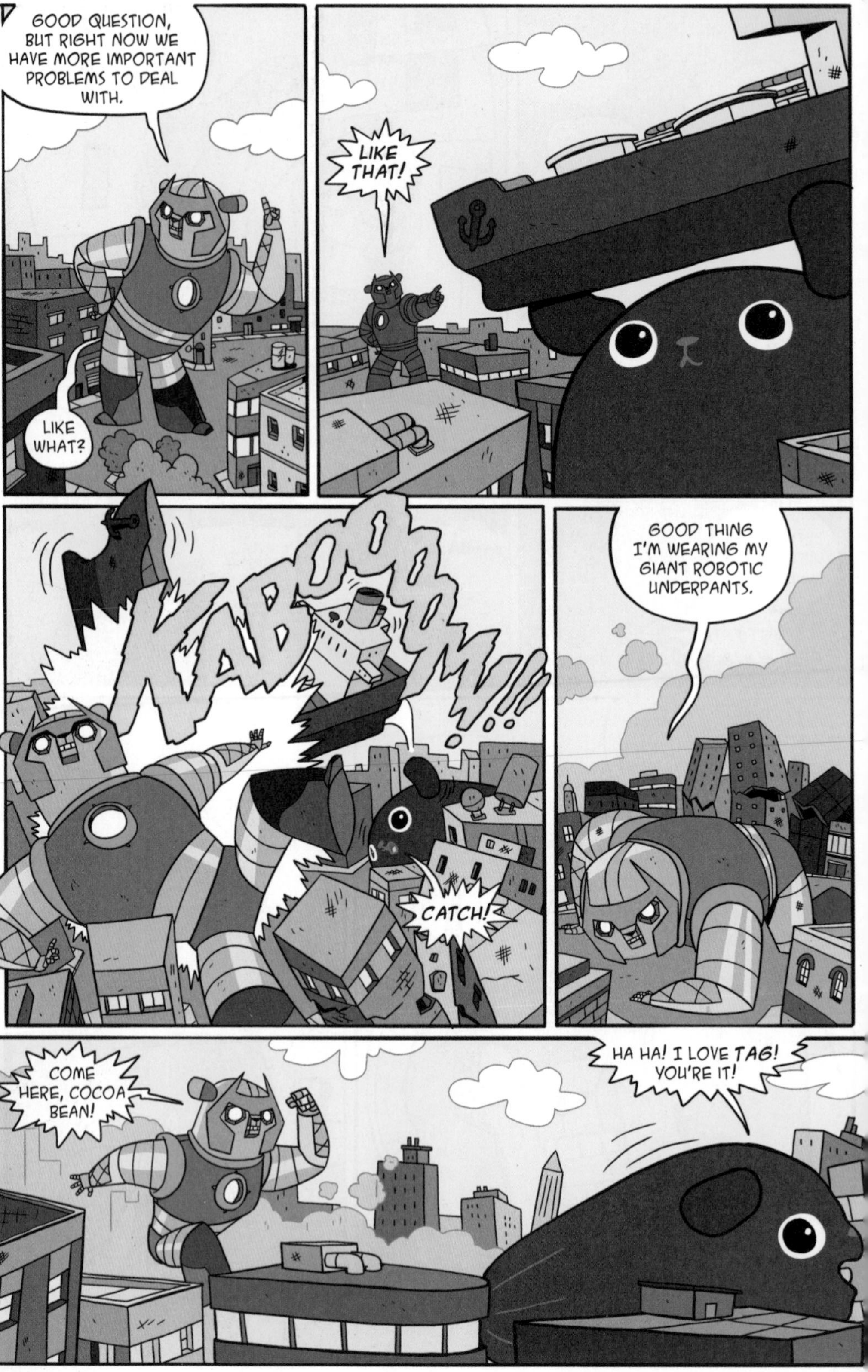
GOOD QUESTION, BUT RIGHT NOW WE HAVE MORE IMPORTANT PROBLEMS TO DEAL WITH.
LIKE WHAT?
LIKE THAT!
KABOOOOM!!!
CATCH!
GOOD THING I'M WEARING MY GIANT ROBOTIC UNDERPANTS.
COME HERE, COCOA BEAN!
HA HA! I LOVE TAG! YOU'RE IT!

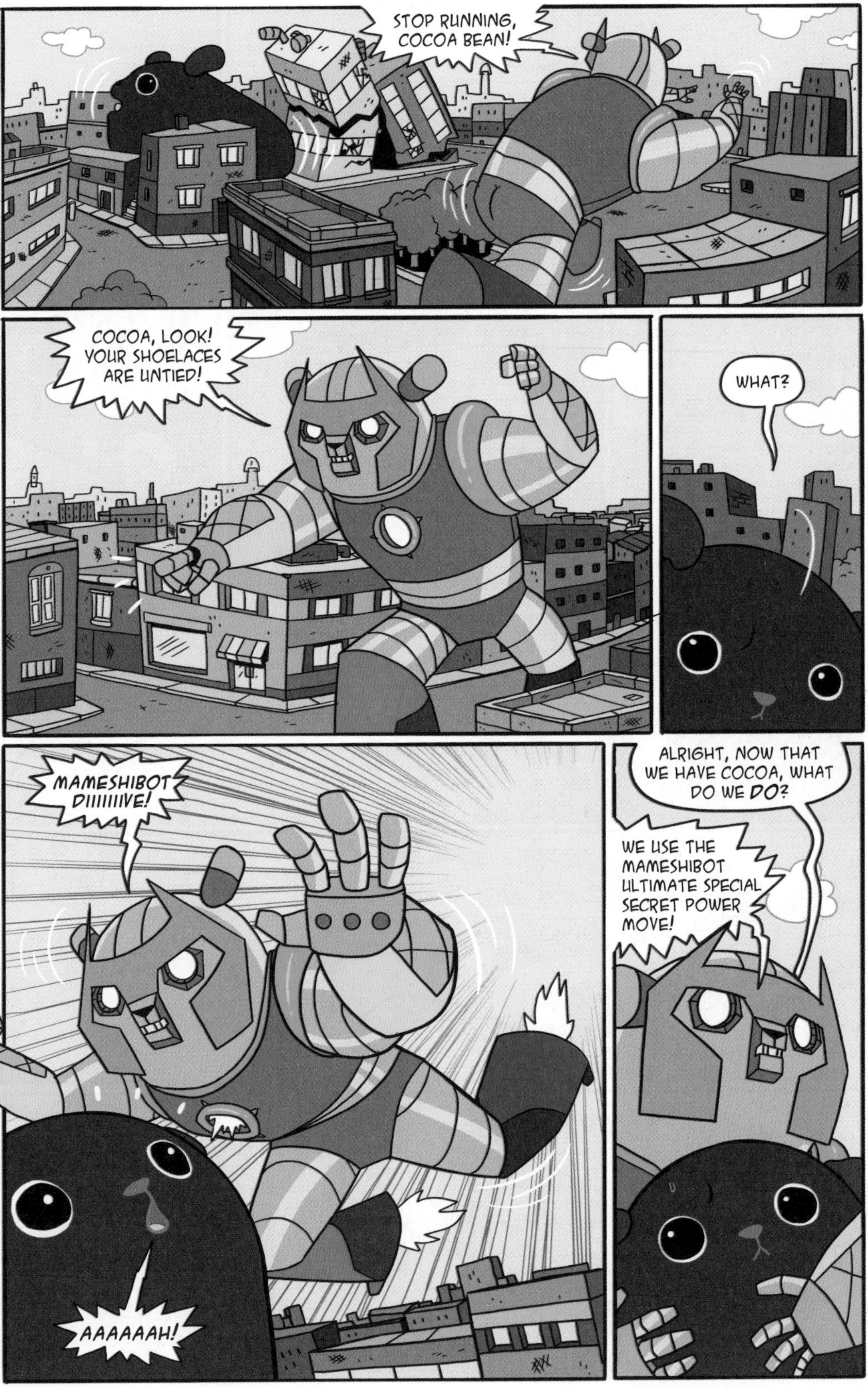
STOP RUNNING, COCOA BEAN!
COCOA, LOOK! YOUR SHOELACES ARE UNTIED!
WHAT?
MAMESHIBOT DIIIIIIIVE!
AAAAAAH!
ALRIGHT, NOW THAT WE HAVE COCOA, WHAT DO WE DO?
WE USE THE MAMESHIBOT ULTIMATE SPECIAL SECRET POWER MOVE!

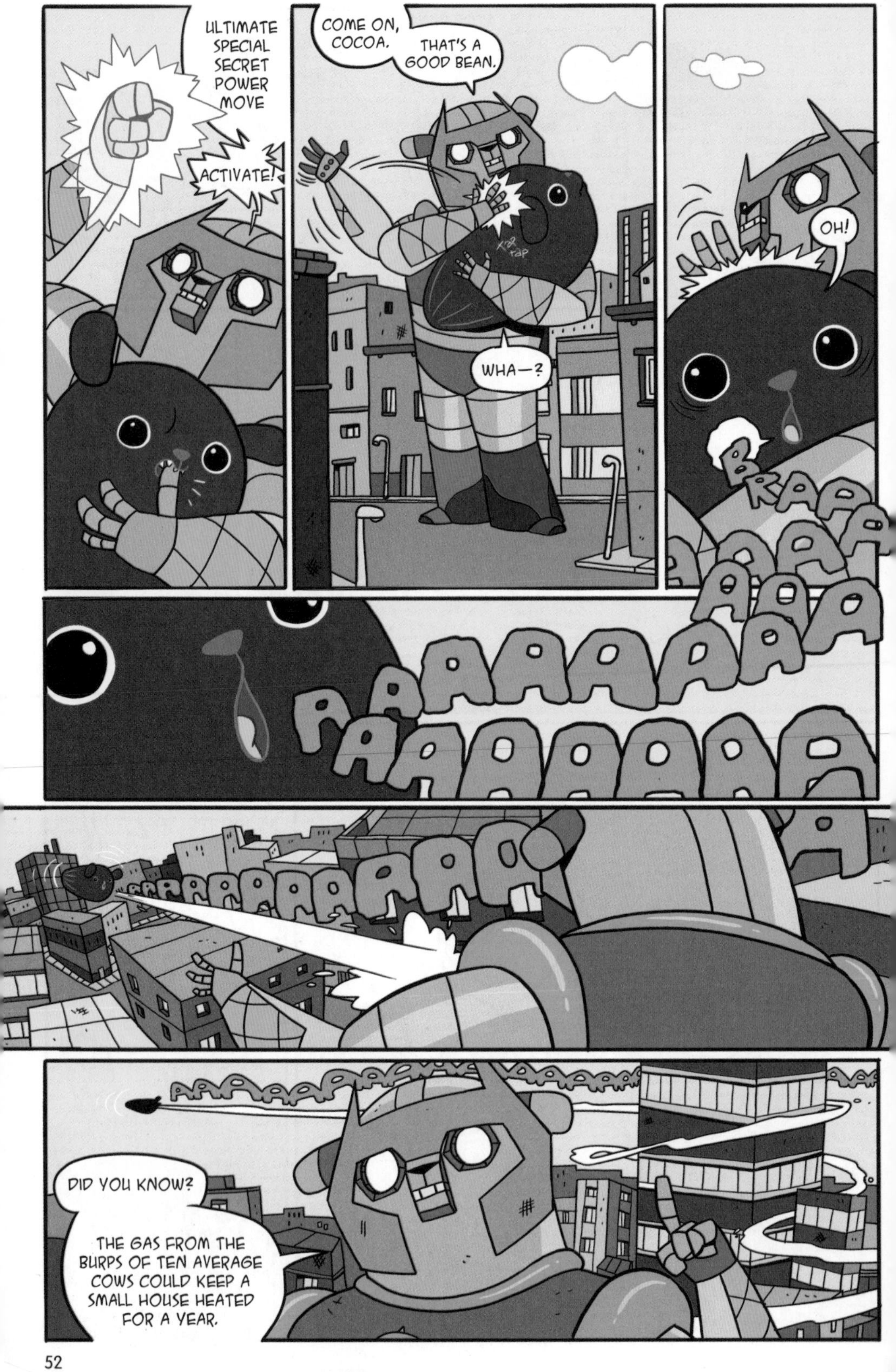
ULTIMATE SPECIAL SECRET POWER MOVE
ACTIVATE!
COME ON, COCOA.
THAT'S A GOOD BEAN.
TAP TAP
WHA—?
OH!
BRAAAAAAAAAAAAAAAAAAAAAAAAAA
DID YOU KNOW?
THE GAS FROM THE BURPS OF TEN AVERAGE COWS COULD KEEP A SMALL HOUSE HEATED FOR A YEAR.

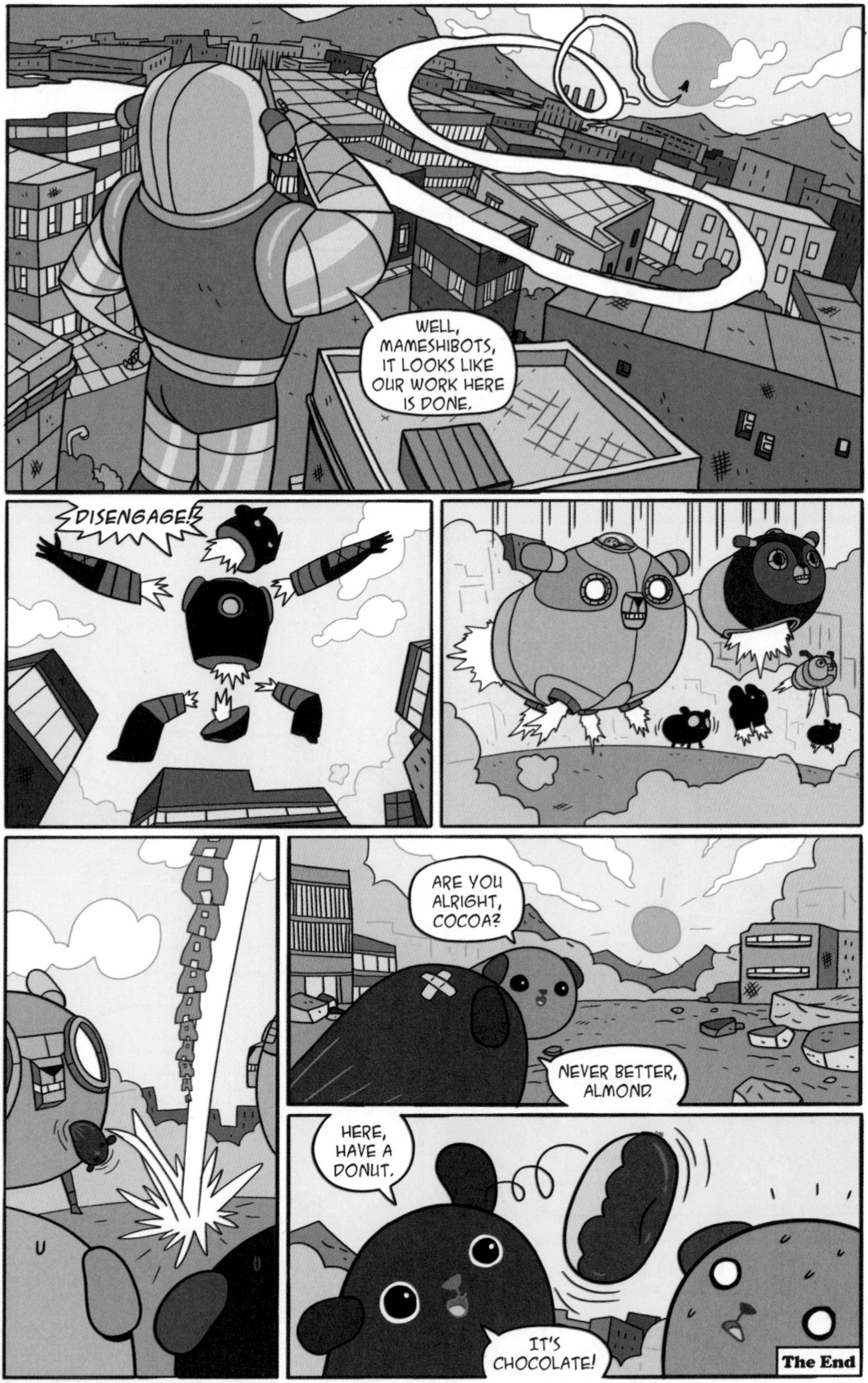
WELL, MAMESHIBOTS, IT LOOKS LIKE OUR WORK HERE IS DONE.
DISENGAGE!
ARE YOU ALRIGHT, COCOA?
NEVER BETTER, ALMOND.
HERE, HAVE A DONUT.
IT'S CHOCOLATE!
The End

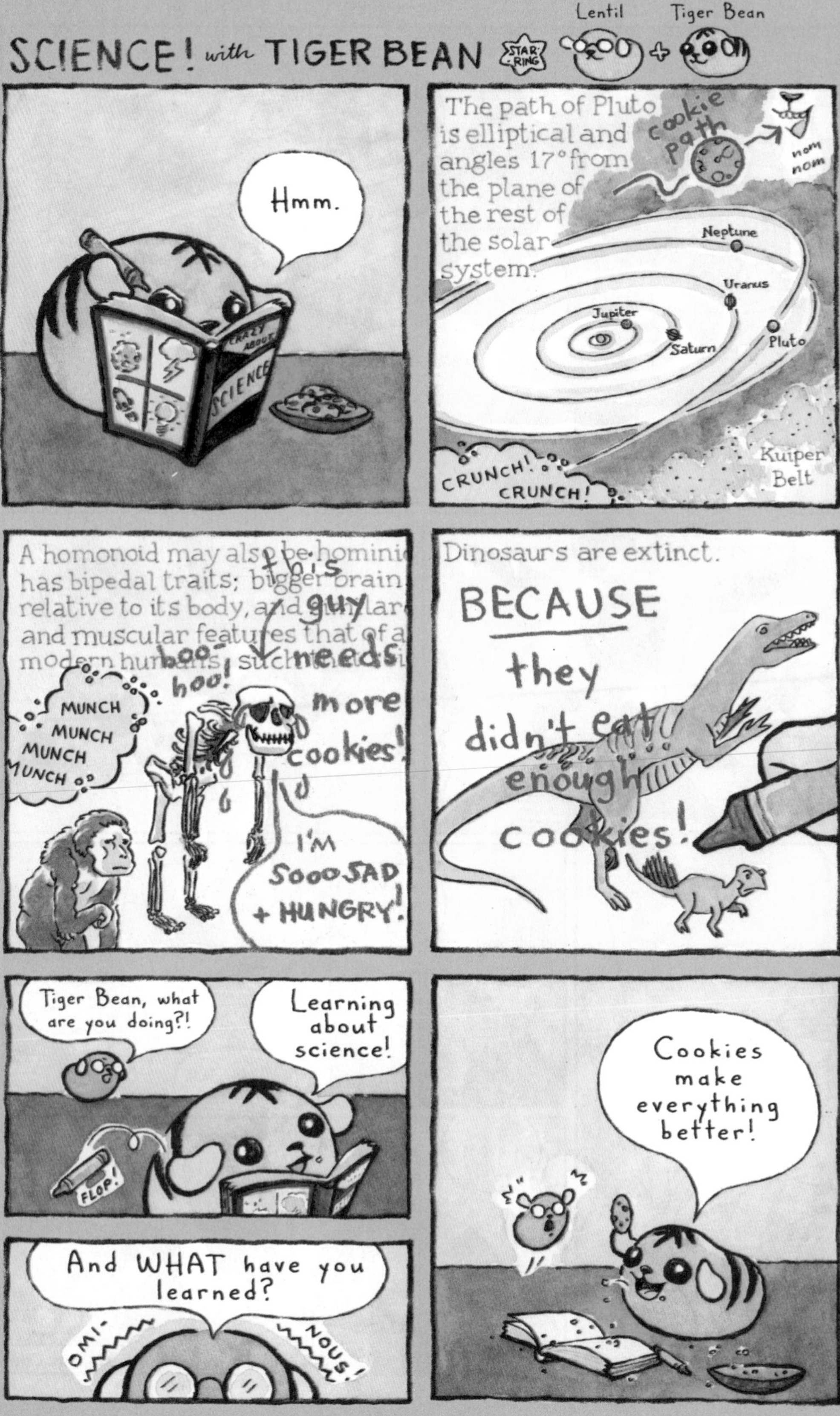
SCIENCE! with TIGER BEAN
STARRING
Lentil
Tiger Bean
Hmm.
CRAZY ABOUT SCIENCE
The path of Pluto is elliptical and angles 17° from the plane of the rest of the solar system.
cookie path
nom nom
Neptune
Uranus
Jupiter
Saturn
Pluto
Kuiper Belt
CRUNCH! CRUNCH!
A homonoid may also be hominid ... has bipedal traits; bigger brain ... relative to its body, and similar ... and muscular features that of a ... modern humans, such ...
this guy needs more cookies!
boo-hoo!
MUNCH MUNCH MUNCH MUNCH
I'M SOOO SAD + HUNGRY!
Dinosaurs are extinct.
BECAUSE they didn't eat enough cookies!
Tiger Bean, what are you doing?!
Learning about science!
FLOP!
And WHAT have you learned?
OMI- NOUS!
Cookies make everything better!

Once Upon a Time...

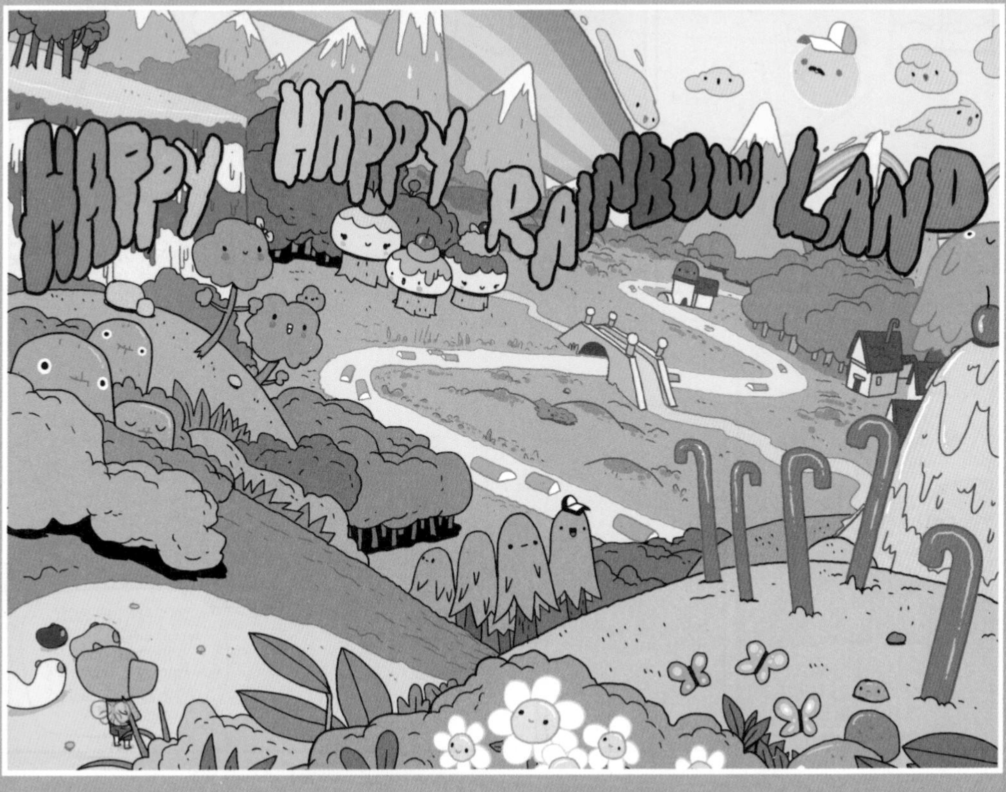
HAPPY HAPPY RAINBOW LAND

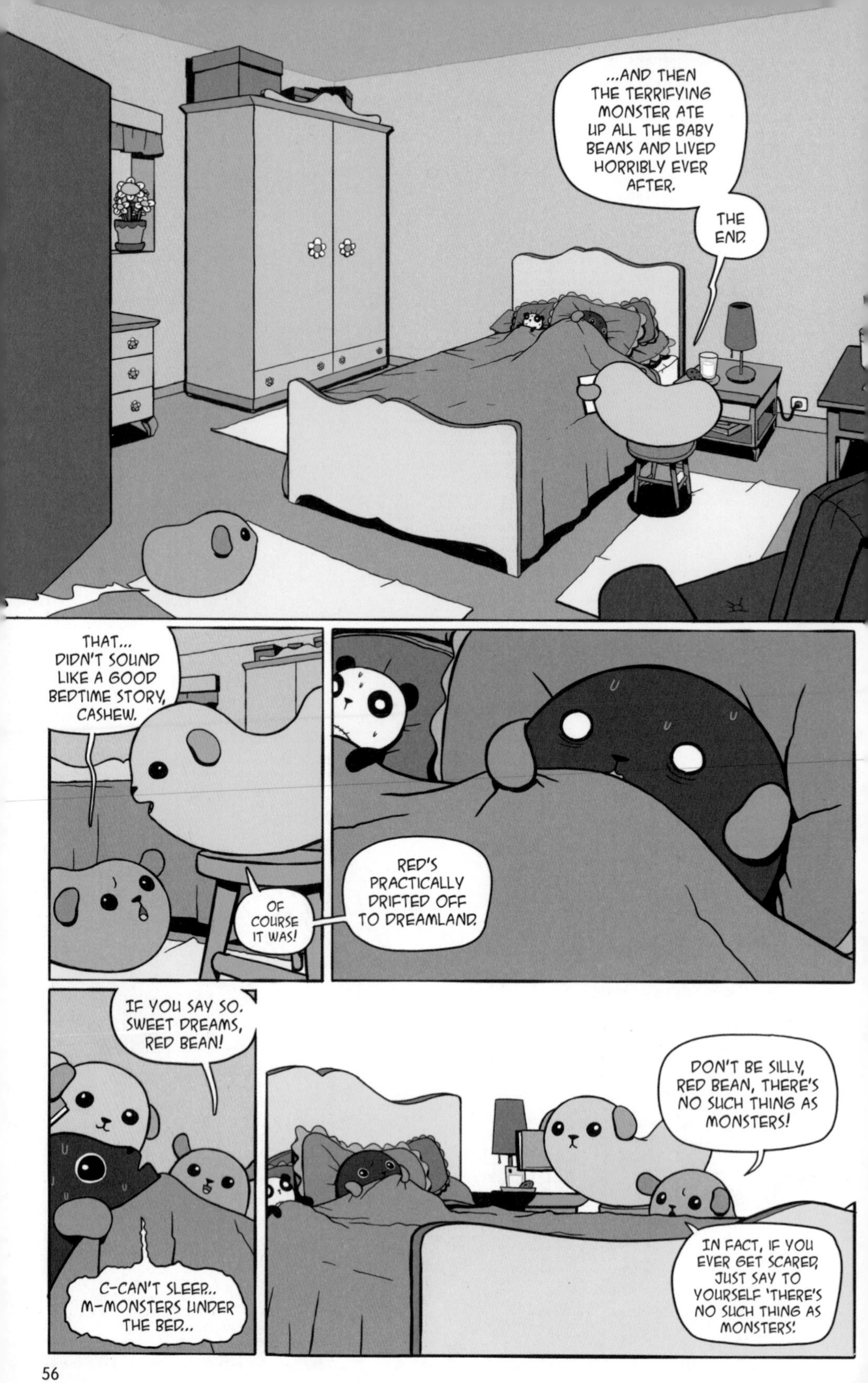
...AND THEN THE TERRIFYING MONSTER ATE UP ALL THE BABY BEANS AND LIVED HORRIBLY EVER AFTER.
THE END.
THAT... DIDN'T SOUND LIKE A GOOD BEDTIME STORY, CASHEW.
OF COURSE IT WAS!
RED'S PRACTICALLY DRIFTED OFF TO DREAMLAND.
IF YOU SAY SO. SWEET DREAMS, RED BEAN!
C-CAN'T SLEEP... M-MONSTERS UNDER THE BED...
DON'T BE SILLY, RED BEAN, THERE'S NO SUCH THING AS MONSTERS!
IN FACT, IF YOU EVER GET SCARED, JUST SAY TO YOURSELF 'THERE'S NO SUCH THING AS MONSTERS!'

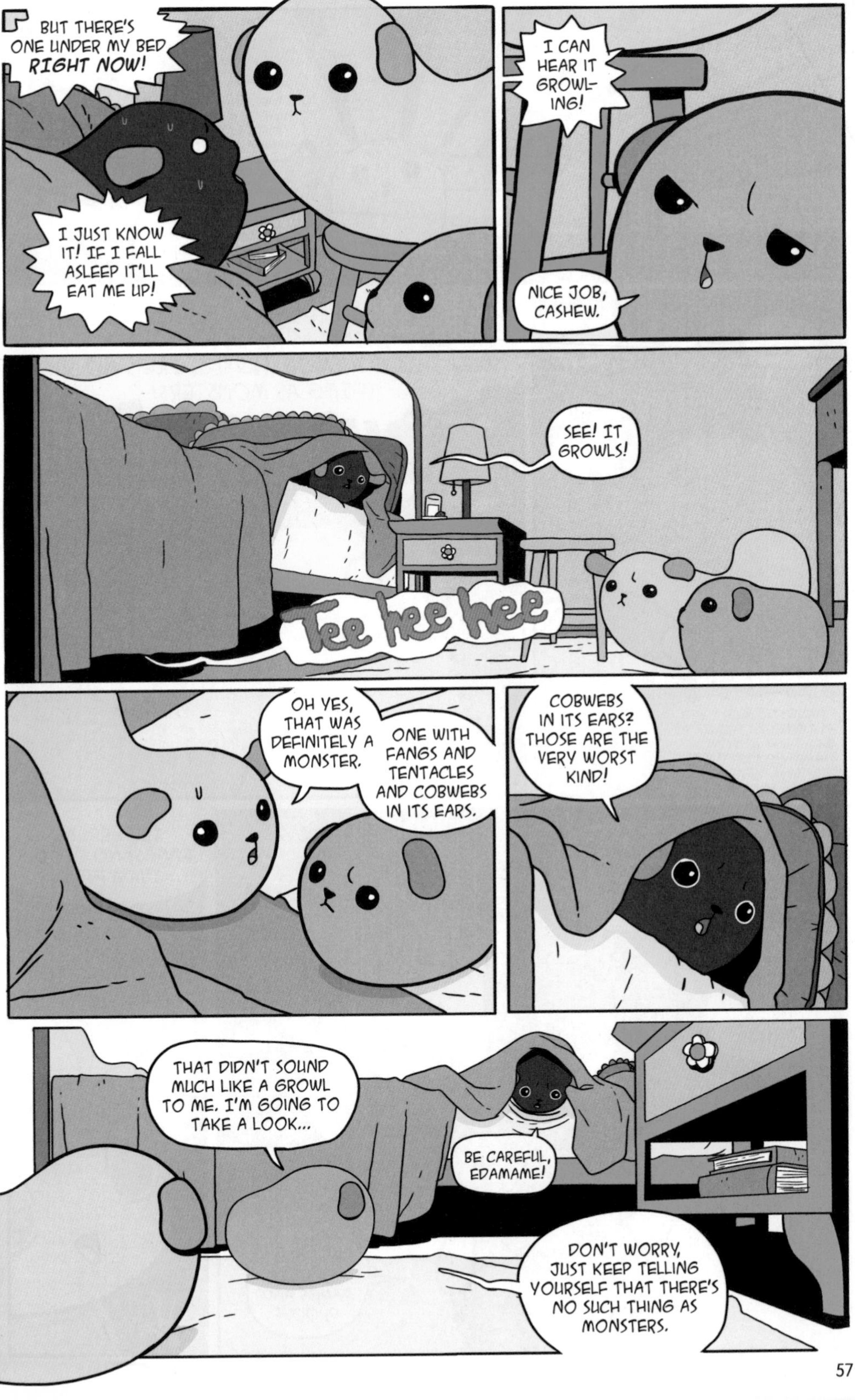
BUT THERE'S ONE UNDER MY BED RIGHT NOW!
I JUST KNOW IT! IF I FALL ASLEEP IT'LL EAT ME UP!
I CAN HEAR IT GROWL-ING!
NICE JOB, CASHEW.
SEE! IT GROWLS!
Tee hee hee
OH YES, THAT WAS DEFINITELY A MONSTER.
ONE WITH FANGS AND TENTACLES AND COBWEBS IN ITS EARS.
COBWEBS IN ITS EARS? THOSE ARE THE VERY WORST KIND!
THAT DIDN'T SOUND MUCH LIKE A GROWL TO ME. I'M GOING TO TAKE A LOOK...
BE CAREFUL, EDAMAME!
DON'T WORRY, JUST KEEP TELLING YOURSELF THAT THERE'S NO SUCH THING AS MONSTERS.

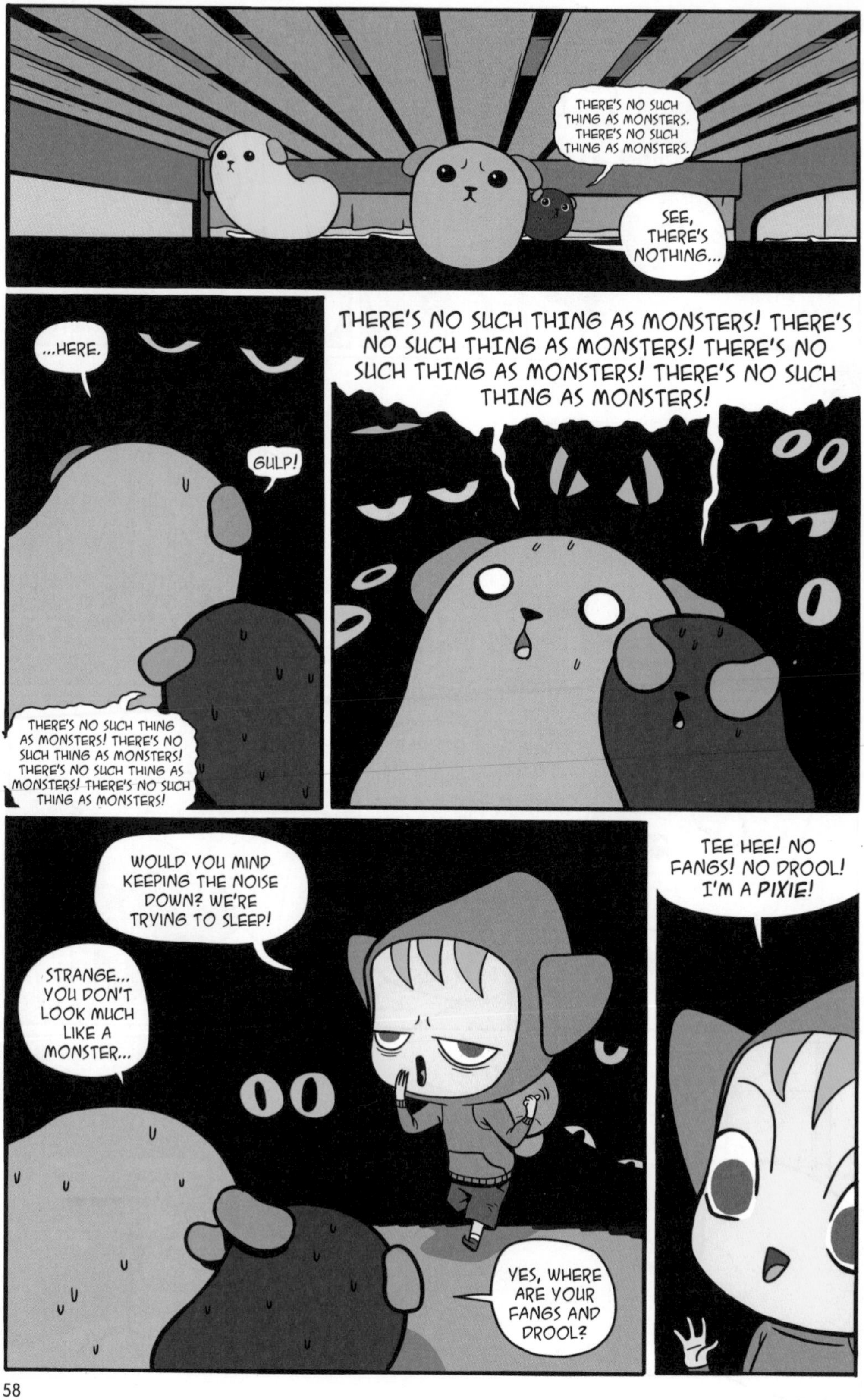
THERE'S NO SUCH THING AS MONSTERS. THERE'S NO SUCH THING AS MONSTERS.
SEE, THERE'S NOTHING...
...HERE.
GULP!
THERE'S NO SUCH THING AS MONSTERS! THERE'S NO SUCH THING AS MONSTERS! THERE'S NO SUCH THING AS MONSTERS! THERE'S NO SUCH THING AS MONSTERS!
THERE'S NO SUCH THING AS MONSTERS! THERE'S NO SUCH THING AS MONSTERS! THERE'S NO SUCH THING AS MONSTERS! THERE'S NO SUCH THING AS MONSTERS!
WOULD YOU MIND KEEPING THE NOISE DOWN? WE'RE TRYING TO SLEEP!
STRANGE... YOU DON'T LOOK MUCH LIKE A MONSTER...
YES, WHERE ARE YOUR FANGS AND DROOL?
TEE HEE! NO FANGS! NO DROOL! I'M A PIXIE!

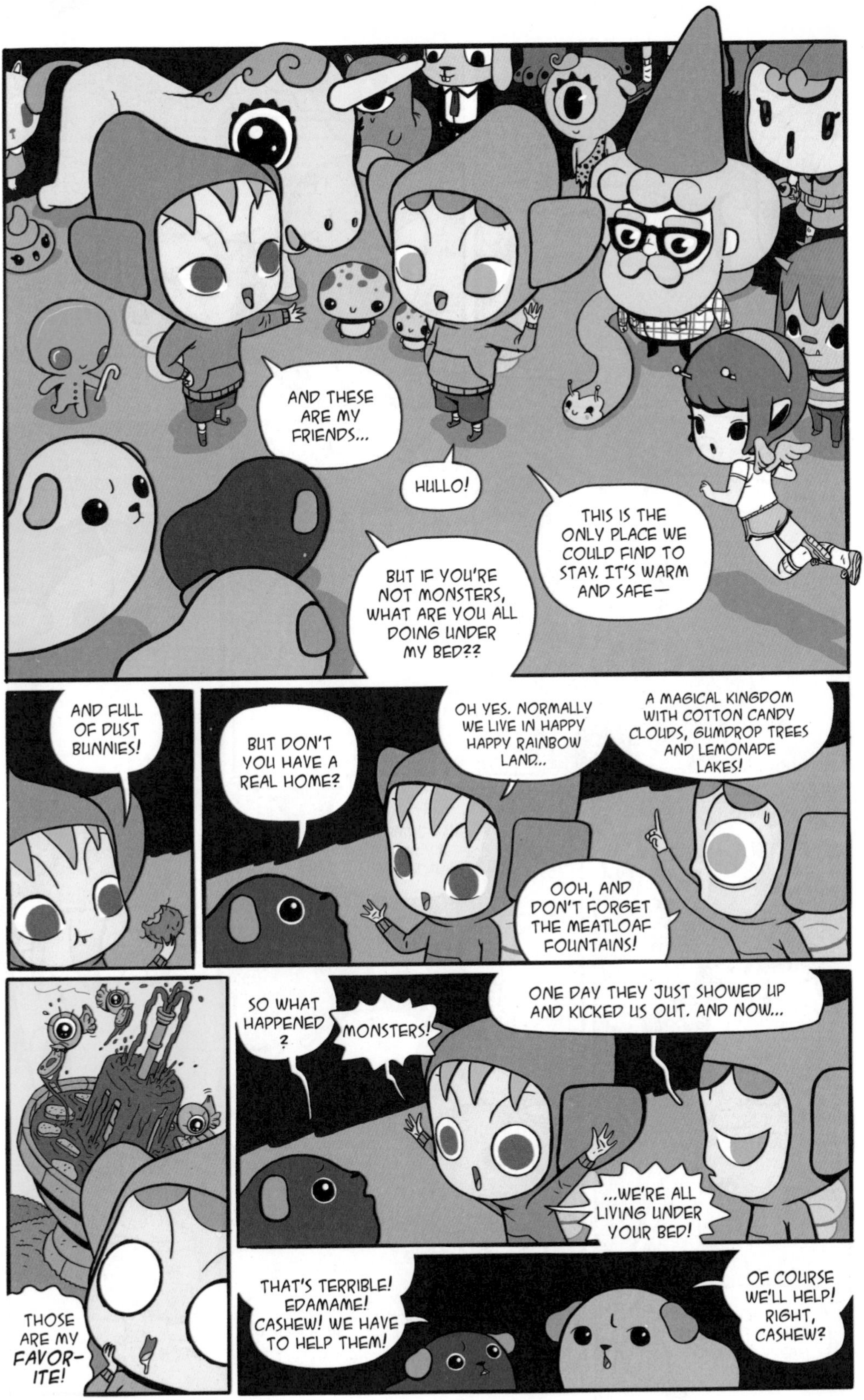
AND THESE ARE MY FRIENDS...
HULLO!
THIS IS THE ONLY PLACE WE COULD FIND TO STAY. IT'S WARM AND SAFE—
BUT IF YOU'RE NOT MONSTERS, WHAT ARE YOU ALL DOING UNDER MY BED??
AND FULL OF DUST BUNNIES!
BUT DON'T YOU HAVE A REAL HOME?
OH YES. NORMALLY WE LIVE IN HAPPY HAPPY RAINBOW LAND...
A MAGICAL KINGDOM WITH COTTON CANDY CLOUDS, GUMDROP TREES AND LEMONADE LAKES!
OOH, AND DON'T FORGET THE MEATLOAF FOUNTAINS!
THOSE ARE MY FAVOR-ITE!
SO WHAT HAPPENED?
MONSTERS!
ONE DAY THEY JUST SHOWED UP AND KICKED US OUT. AND NOW...
...WE'RE ALL LIVING UNDER YOUR BED!
THAT'S TERRIBLE! EDAMAME! CASHEW! WE HAVE TO HELP THEM!
OF COURSE WE'LL HELP! RIGHT, CASHEW?

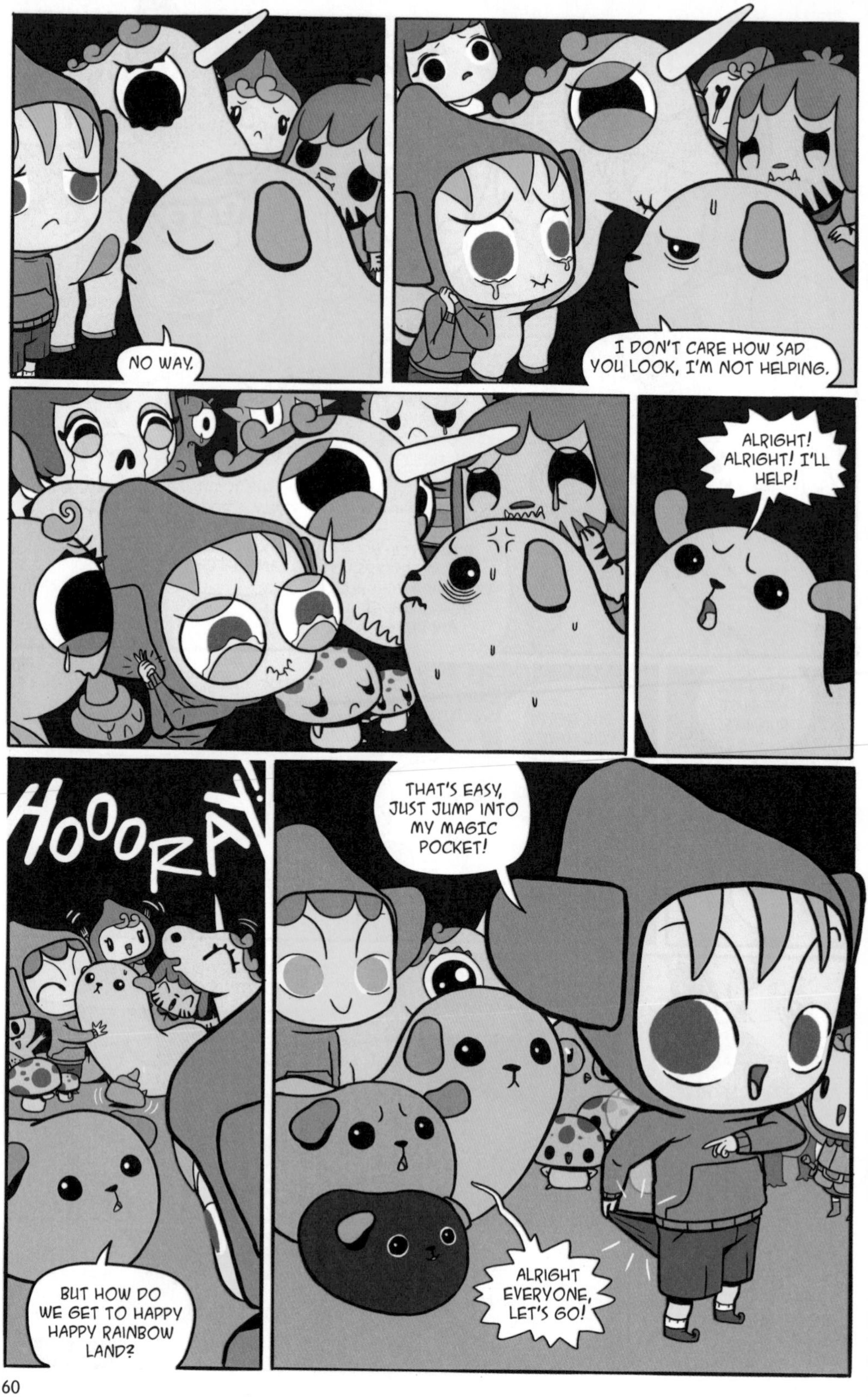
NO WAY.
I DON'T CARE HOW SAD YOU LOOK, I'M NOT HELPING.
ALRIGHT! ALRIGHT! I'LL HELP!
HOOORAY!
BUT HOW DO WE GET TO HAPPY HAPPY RAINBOW LAND?
THAT'S EASY, JUST JUMP INTO MY MAGIC POCKET!
ALRIGHT EVERYONE, LET'S GO!

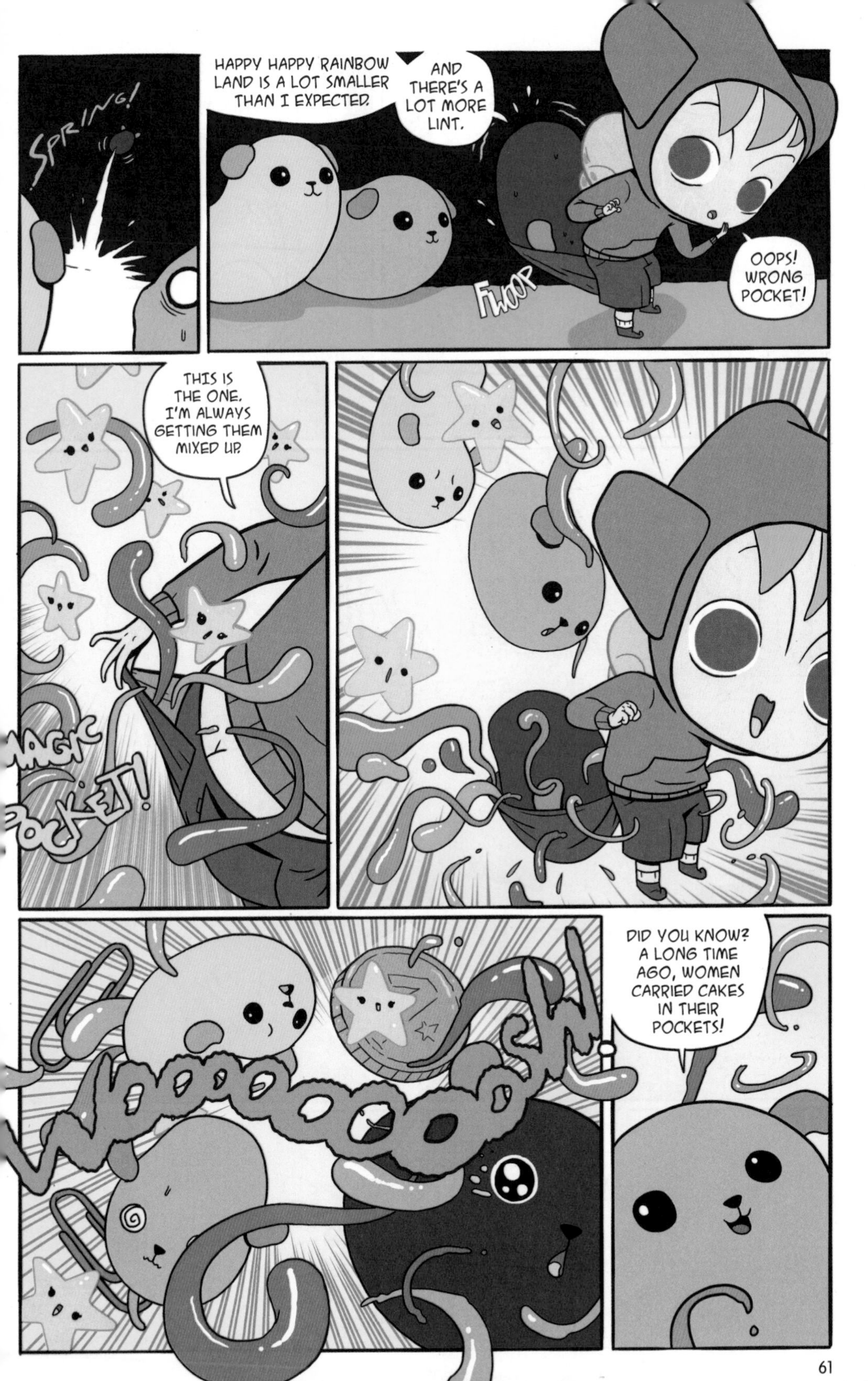
SPRING!
HAPPY HAPPY RAINBOW LAND IS A LOT SMALLER THAN I EXPECTED.
AND THERE'S A LOT MORE LINT.
FWOOP
OOPS! WRONG POCKET!
THIS IS THE ONE. I'M ALWAYS GETTING THEM MIXED UP.
MAGIC POCKET!
WOOOOOOOSH!
DID YOU KNOW? A LONG TIME AGO, WOMEN CARRIED CAKES IN THEIR POCKETS!

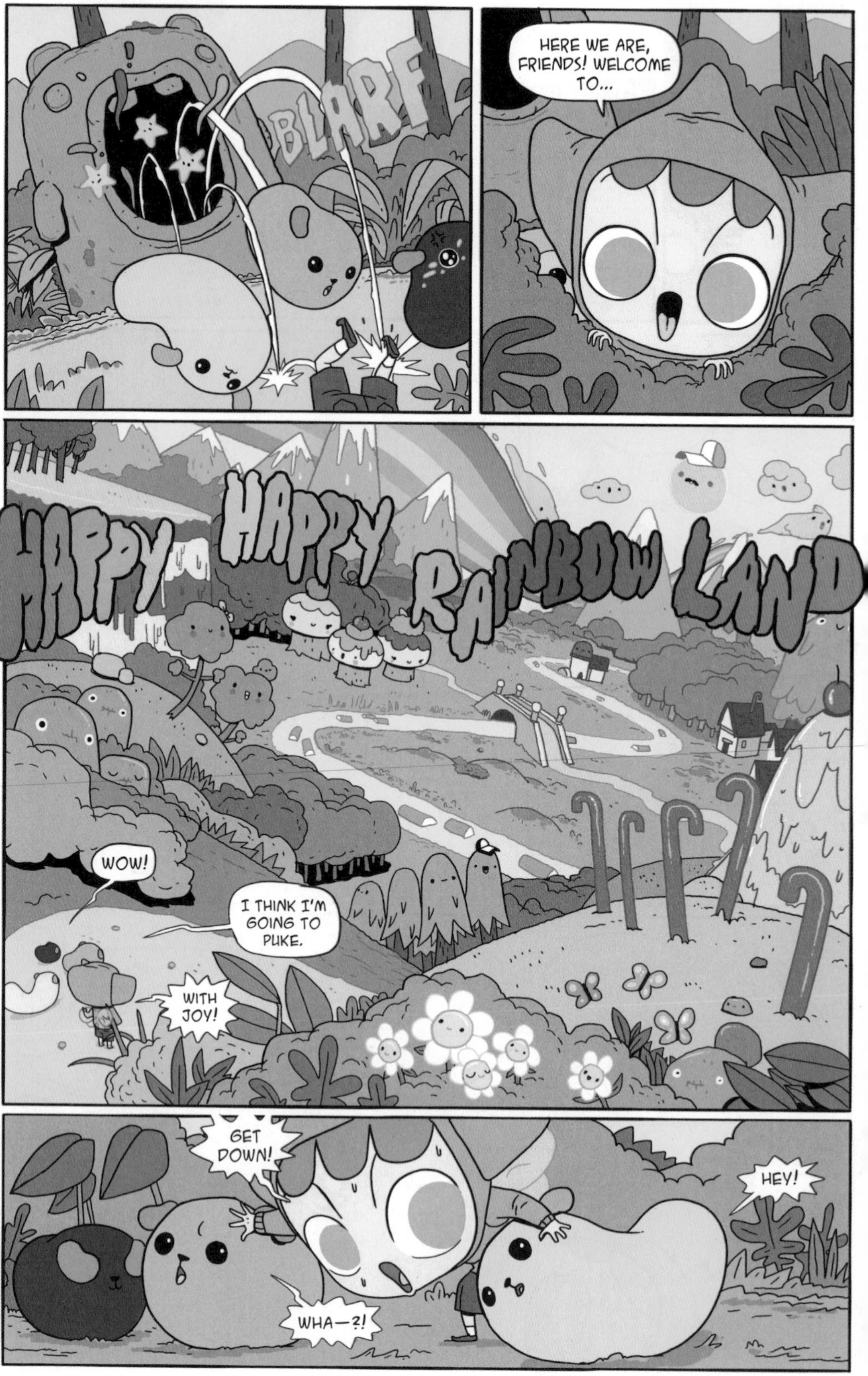
BLARF
HERE WE ARE, FRIENDS! WELCOME TO...
HAPPY HAPPY RAINBOW LAND
WOW!
I THINK I'M GOING TO PUKE.
WITH JOY!
GET DOWN!
HEY!
WHA—?!

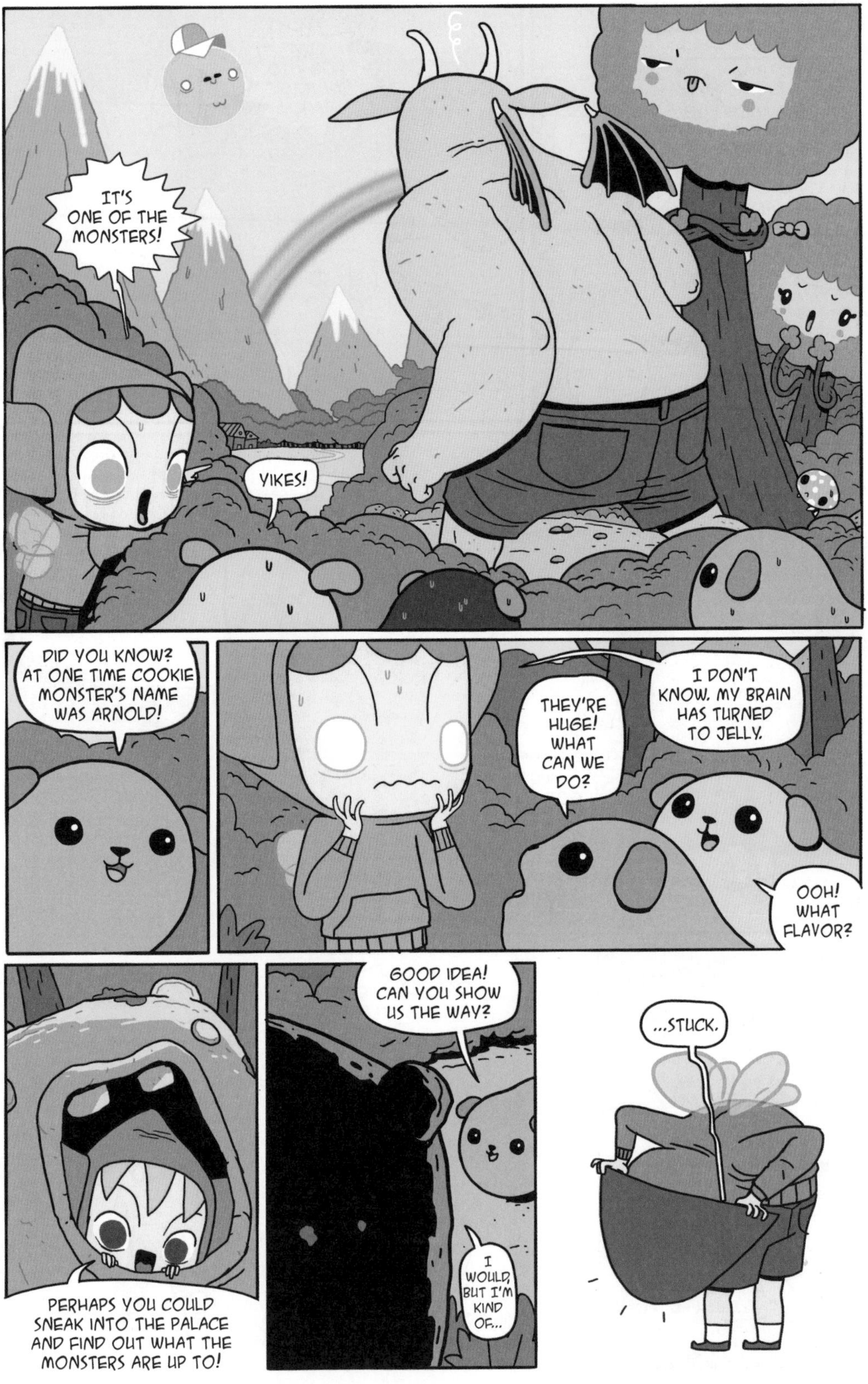
IT'S ONE OF THE MONSTERS!
YIKES!
DID YOU KNOW? AT ONE TIME COOKIE MONSTER'S NAME WAS ARNOLD!
THEY'RE HUGE! WHAT CAN WE DO?
I DON'T KNOW. MY BRAIN HAS TURNED TO JELLY.
OOH! WHAT FLAVOR?
PERHAPS YOU COULD SNEAK INTO THE PALACE AND FIND OUT WHAT THE MONSTERS ARE UP TO!
GOOD IDEA! CAN YOU SHOW US THE WAY?
I WOULD, BUT I'M KIND OF...
...STUCK.

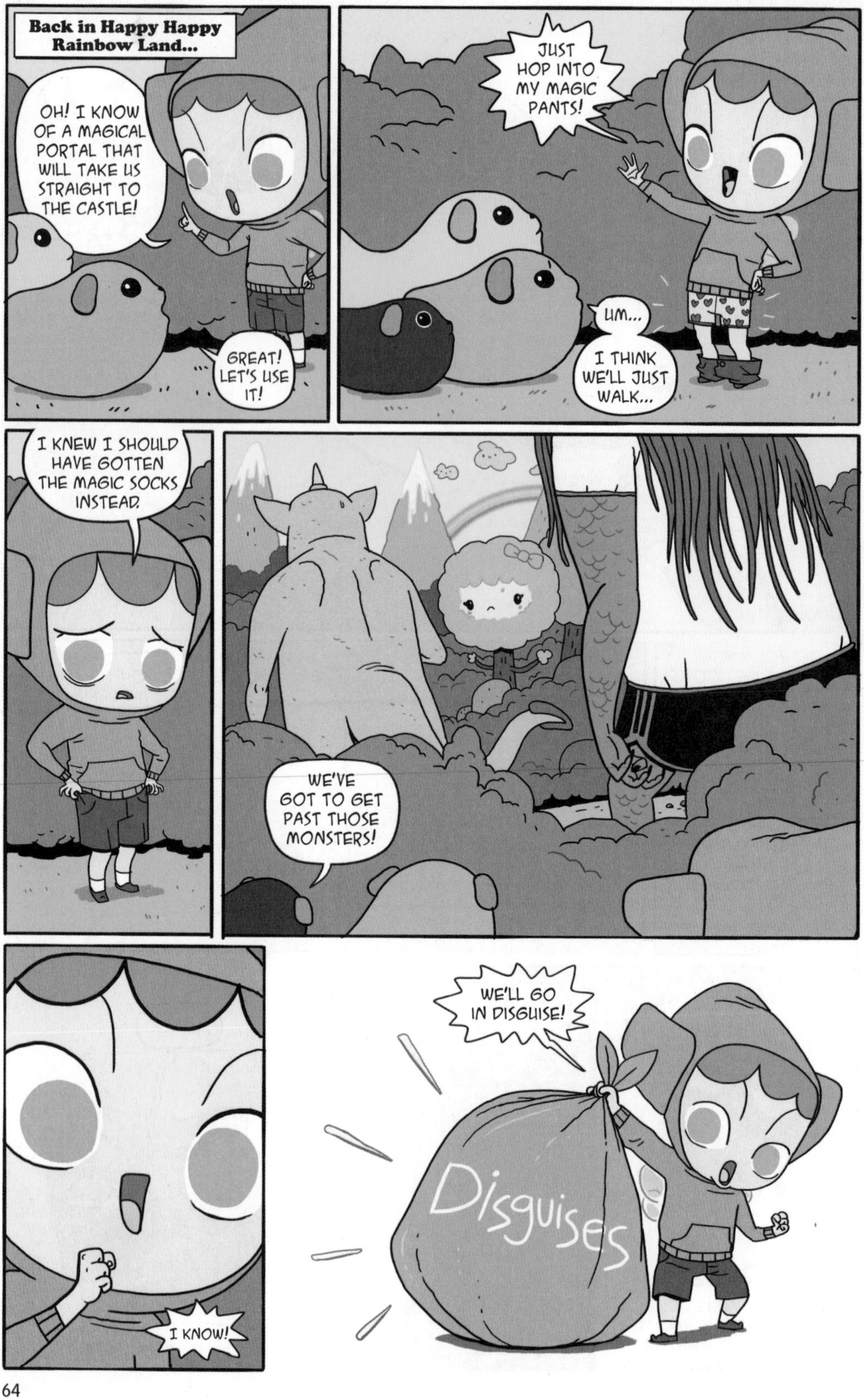
Back in Happy Happy Rainbow Land...
OH! I KNOW OF A MAGICAL PORTAL THAT WILL TAKE US STRAIGHT TO THE CASTLE!
GREAT! LET'S USE IT!
JUST HOP INTO MY MAGIC PANTS!
UM...
I THINK WE'LL JUST WALK...
I KNEW I SHOULD HAVE GOTTEN THE MAGIC SOCKS INSTEAD.
WE'VE GOT TO GET PAST THOSE MONSTERS!
I KNOW!
WE'LL GO IN DISGUISE!
Disguises

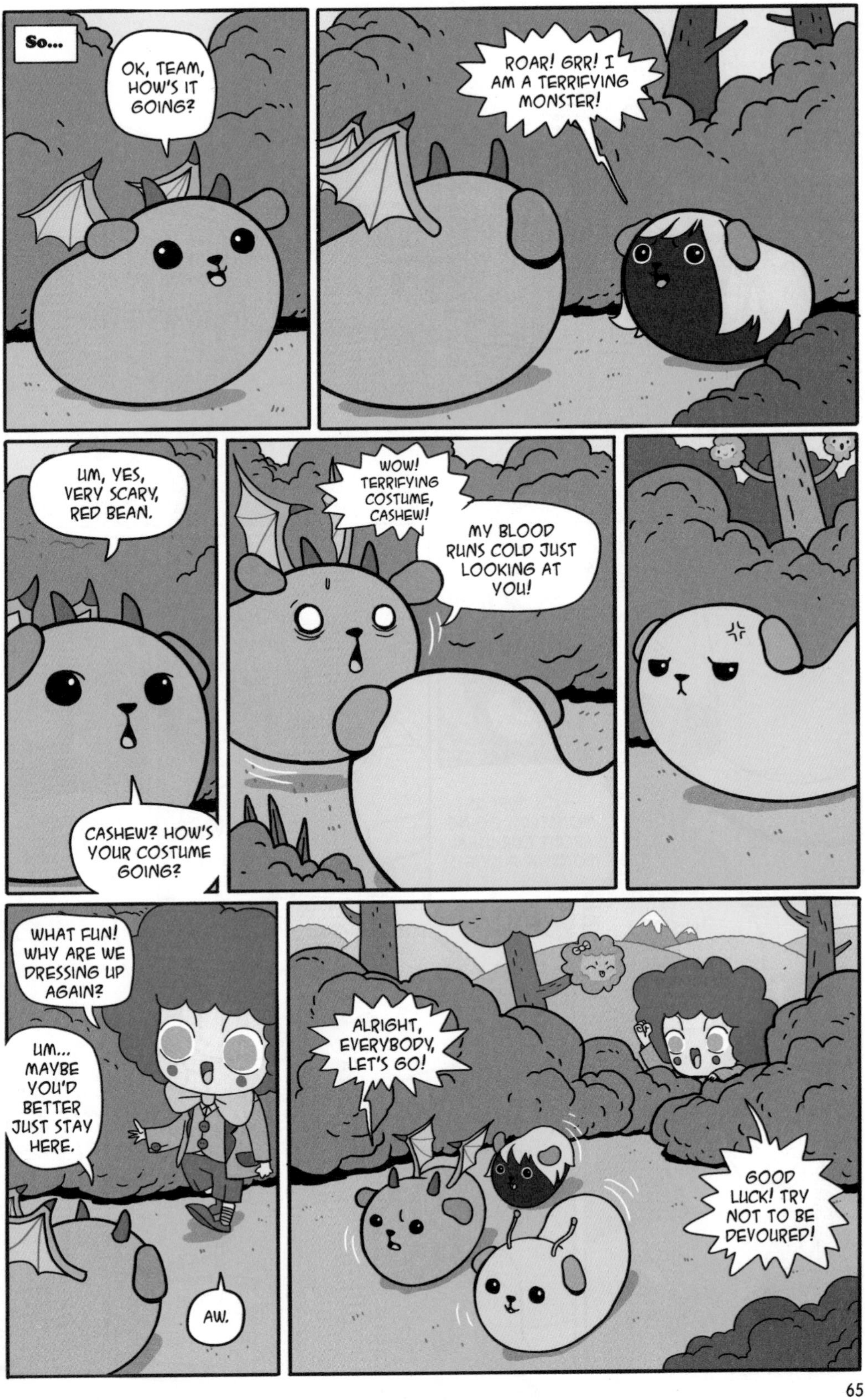
So...
OK, TEAM, HOW'S IT GOING?
ROAR! GRR! I AM A TERRIFYING MONSTER!
UM, YES, VERY SCARY, RED BEAN.
CASHEW? HOW'S YOUR COSTUME GOING?
WOW! TERRIFYING COSTUME, CASHEW!
MY BLOOD RUNS COLD JUST LOOKING AT YOU!
WHAT FUN! WHY ARE WE DRESSING UP AGAIN?
UM... MAYBE YOU'D BETTER JUST STAY HERE.
AW.
ALRIGHT, EVERYBODY, LET'S GO!
GOOD LUCK! TRY NOT TO BE DEVOURED!

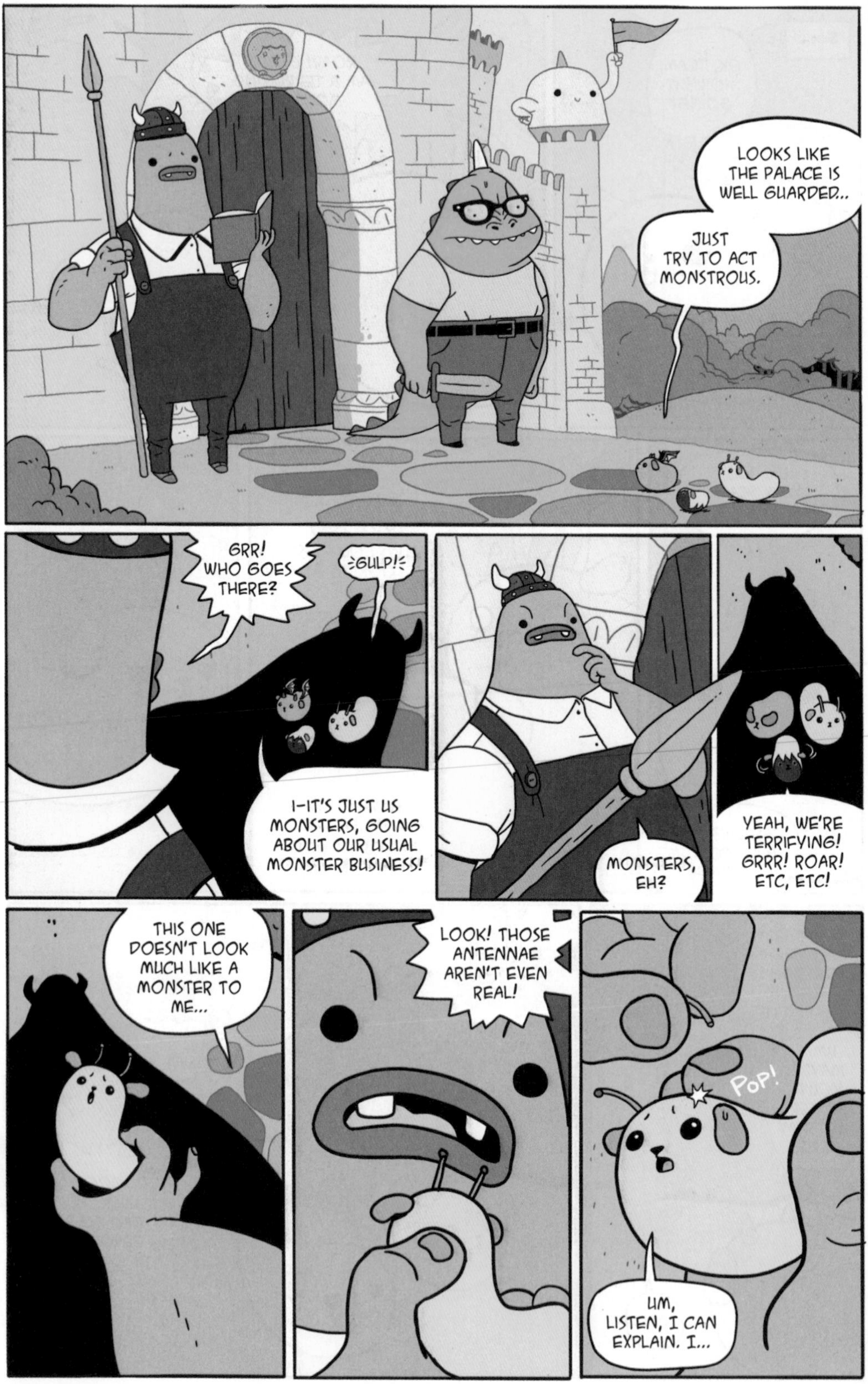
LOOKS LIKE THE PALACE IS WELL GUARDED...
JUST TRY TO ACT MONSTROUS.
GRR! WHO GOES THERE?
GULP!
I-IT'S JUST US MONSTERS, GOING ABOUT OUR USUAL MONSTER BUSINESS!
MONSTERS, EH?
YEAH, WE'RE TERRIFYING! GRRR! ROAR! ETC, ETC!
THIS ONE DOESN'T LOOK MUCH LIKE A MONSTER TO ME...
LOOK! THOSE ANTENNAE AREN'T EVEN REAL!
POP!
UM, LISTEN, I CAN EXPLAIN. I...

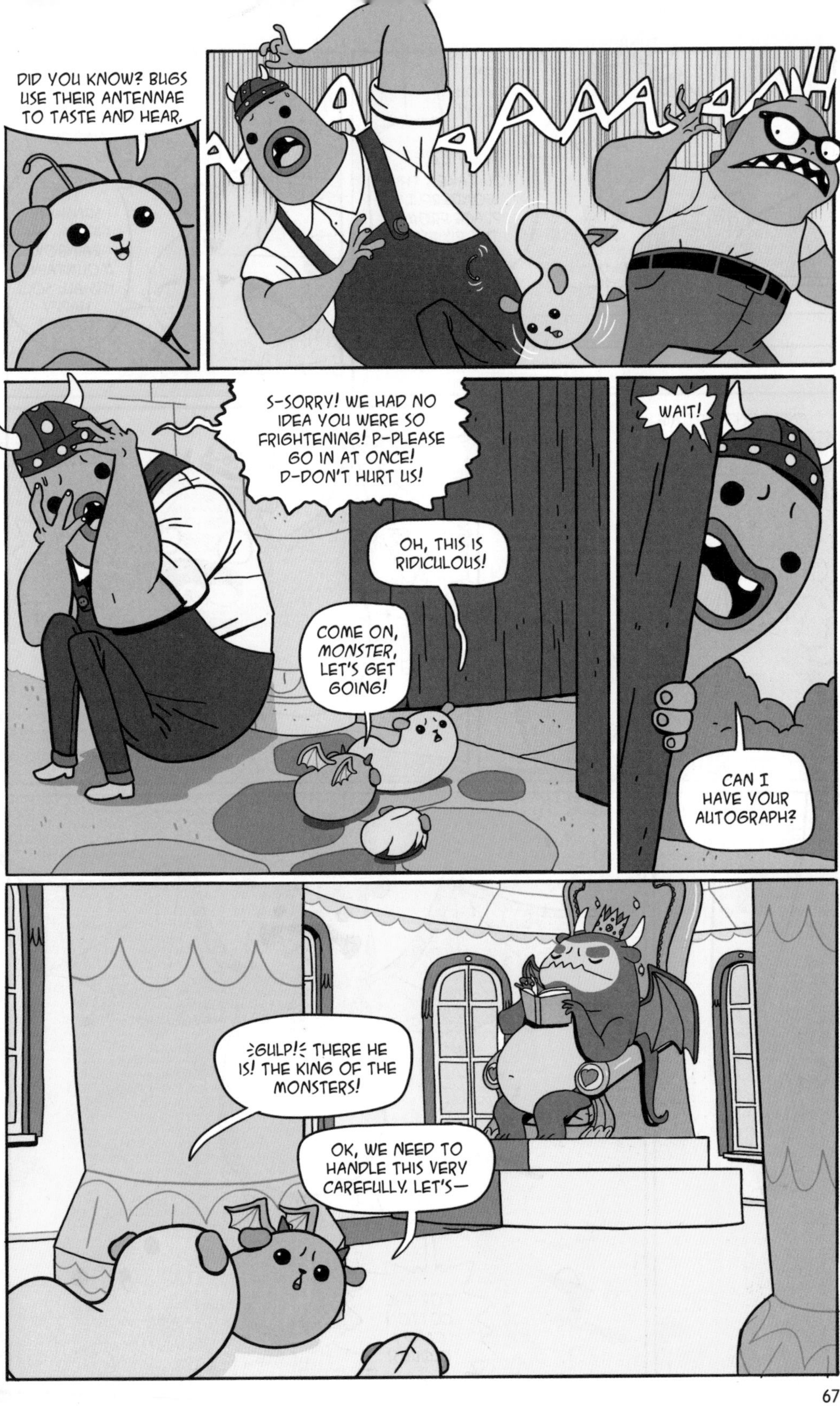
DID YOU KNOW? BUGS USE THEIR ANTENNAE TO TASTE AND HEAR.
AAAAAAAAAAAAH
S-SORRY! WE HAD NO IDEA YOU WERE SO FRIGHTENING! P-PLEASE GO IN AT ONCE! D-DON'T HURT US!
OH, THIS IS RIDICULOUS!
COME ON, MONSTER, LET'S GET GOING!
WAIT!
CAN I HAVE YOUR AUTOGRAPH?
GULP! THERE HE IS! THE KING OF THE MONSTERS!
OK, WE NEED TO HANDLE THIS VERY CAREFULLY. LET'S—

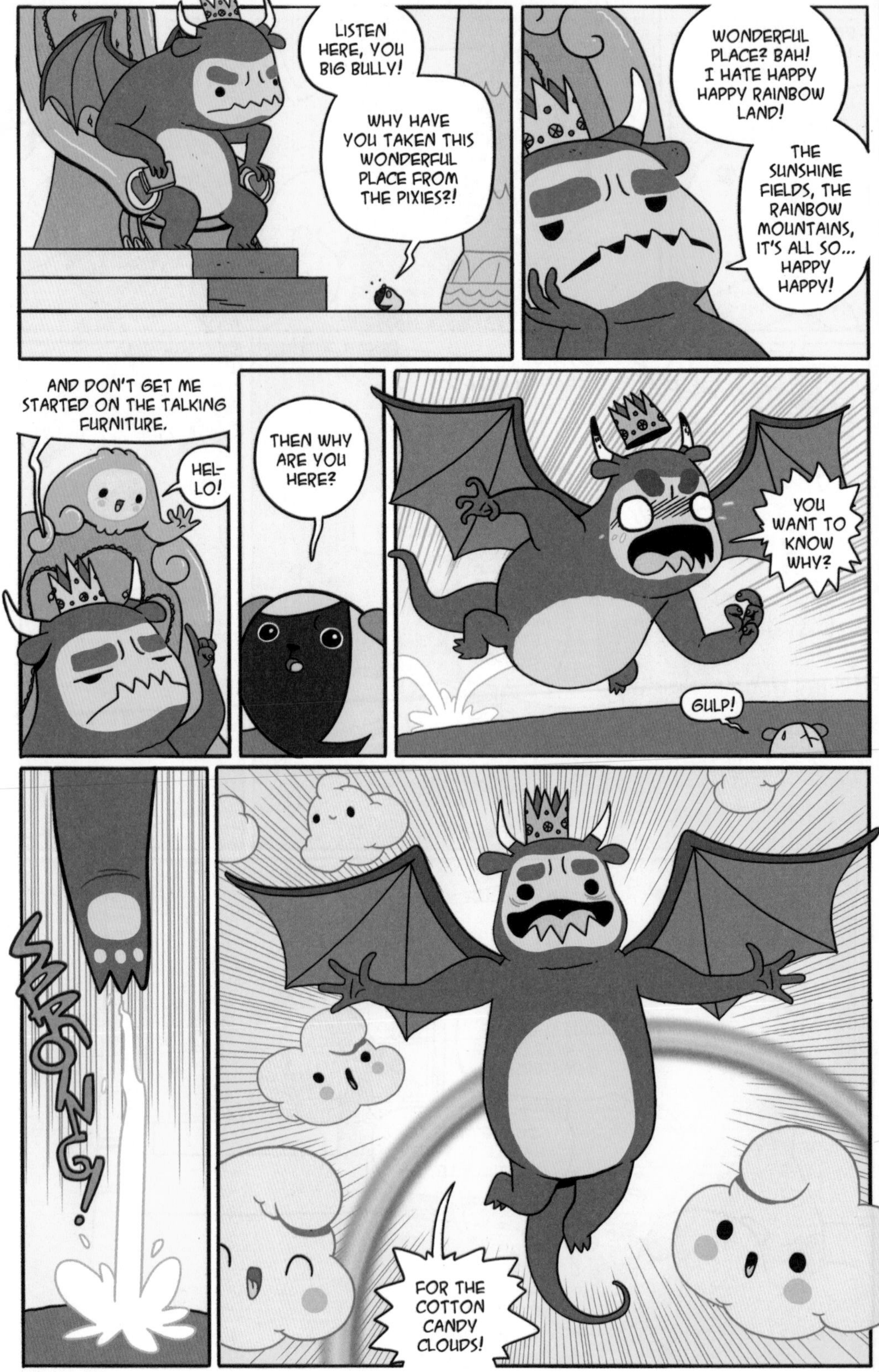
LISTEN HERE, YOU BIG BULLY!
WHY HAVE YOU TAKEN THIS WONDERFUL PLACE FROM THE PIXIES?!
WONDERFUL PLACE? BAH! I HATE HAPPY HAPPY RAINBOW LAND!
THE SUNSHINE FIELDS, THE RAINBOW MOUNTAINS, IT'S ALL SO... HAPPY HAPPY!
AND DON'T GET ME STARTED ON THE TALKING FURNITURE.
HEL-LO!
THEN WHY ARE YOU HERE?
YOU WANT TO KNOW WHY?
GULP!
FOR THE COTTON CANDY CLOUDS!

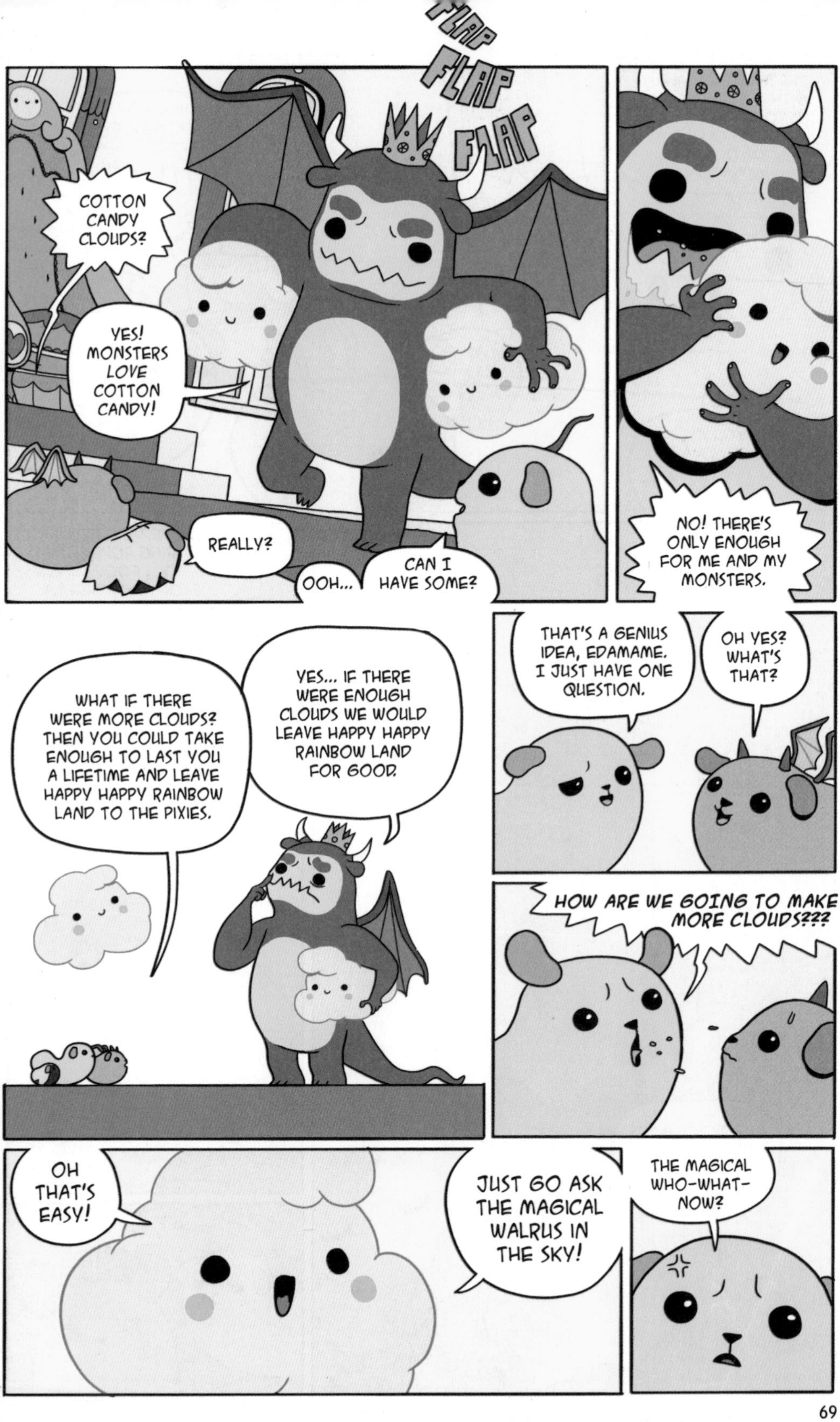
FLAP
FLAP
FLAP
COTTON CANDY CLOUDS?
YES! MONSTERS LOVE COTTON CANDY!
REALLY?
OOH...
CAN I HAVE SOME?
NO! THERE'S ONLY ENOUGH FOR ME AND MY MONSTERS.
WHAT IF THERE WERE MORE CLOUDS? THEN YOU COULD TAKE ENOUGH TO LAST YOU A LIFETIME AND LEAVE HAPPY HAPPY RAINBOW LAND TO THE PIXIES.
YES... IF THERE WERE ENOUGH CLOUDS WE WOULD LEAVE HAPPY HAPPY RAINBOW LAND FOR GOOD.
THAT'S A GENIUS IDEA, EDAMAME. I JUST HAVE ONE QUESTION.
OH YES? WHAT'S THAT?
HOW ARE WE GOING TO MAKE MORE CLOUDS???
OH THAT'S EASY!
JUST GO ASK THE MAGICAL WALRUS IN THE SKY!
THE MAGICAL WHO-WHAT-NOW?

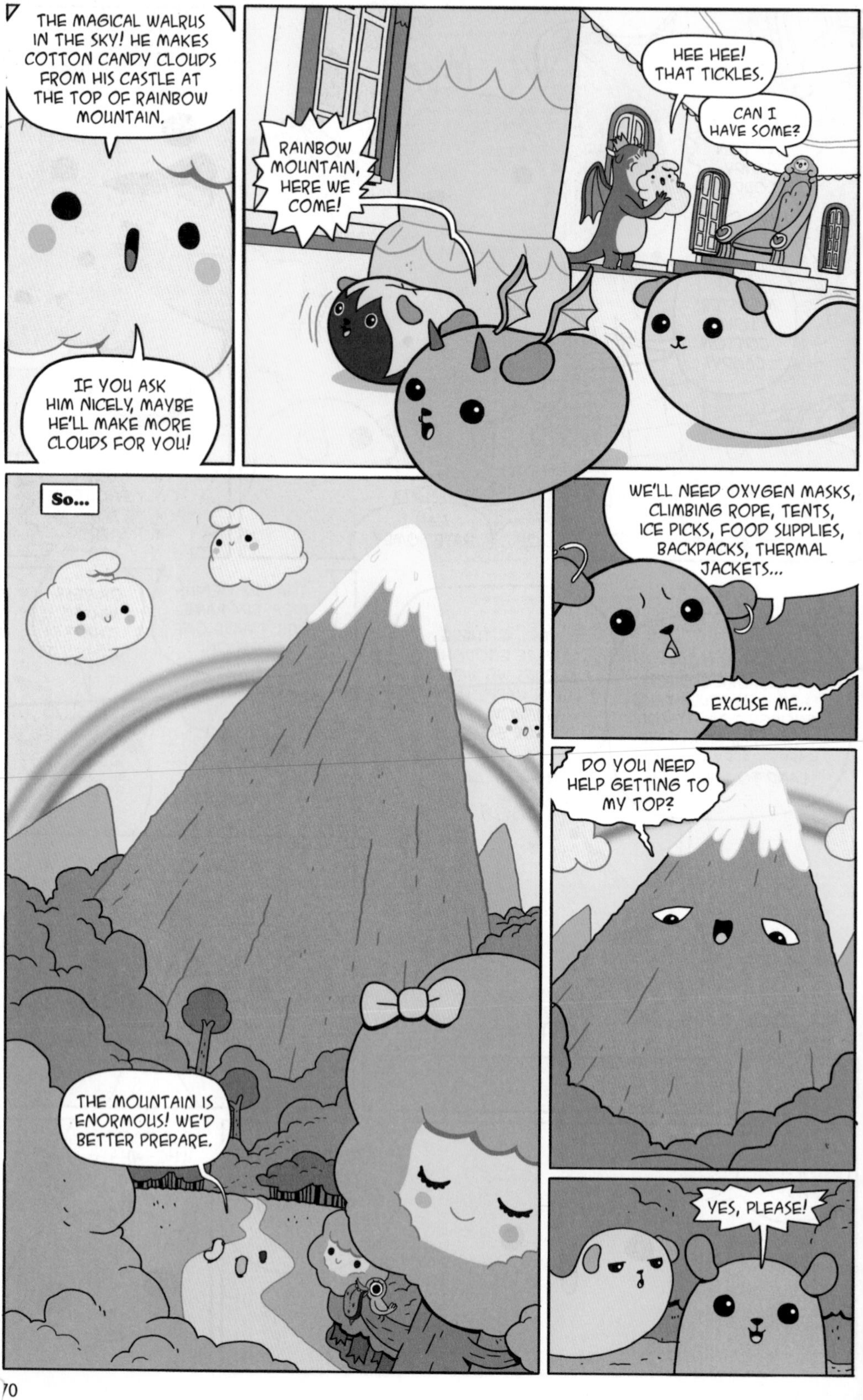
THE MAGICAL WALRUS IN THE SKY! HE MAKES COTTON CANDY CLOUDS FROM HIS CASTLE AT THE TOP OF RAINBOW MOUNTAIN.
IF YOU ASK HIM NICELY, MAYBE HE'LL MAKE MORE CLOUDS FOR YOU!
HEE HEE! THAT TICKLES.
CAN I HAVE SOME?
RAINBOW MOUNTAIN, HERE WE COME!
So...
THE MOUNTAIN IS ENORMOUS! WE'D BETTER PREPARE.
WE'LL NEED OXYGEN MASKS, CLIMBING ROPE, TENTS, ICE PICKS, FOOD SUPPLIES, BACKPACKS, THERMAL JACKETS...
EXCUSE ME...
DO YOU NEED HELP GETTING TO MY TOP?
YES, PLEASE!

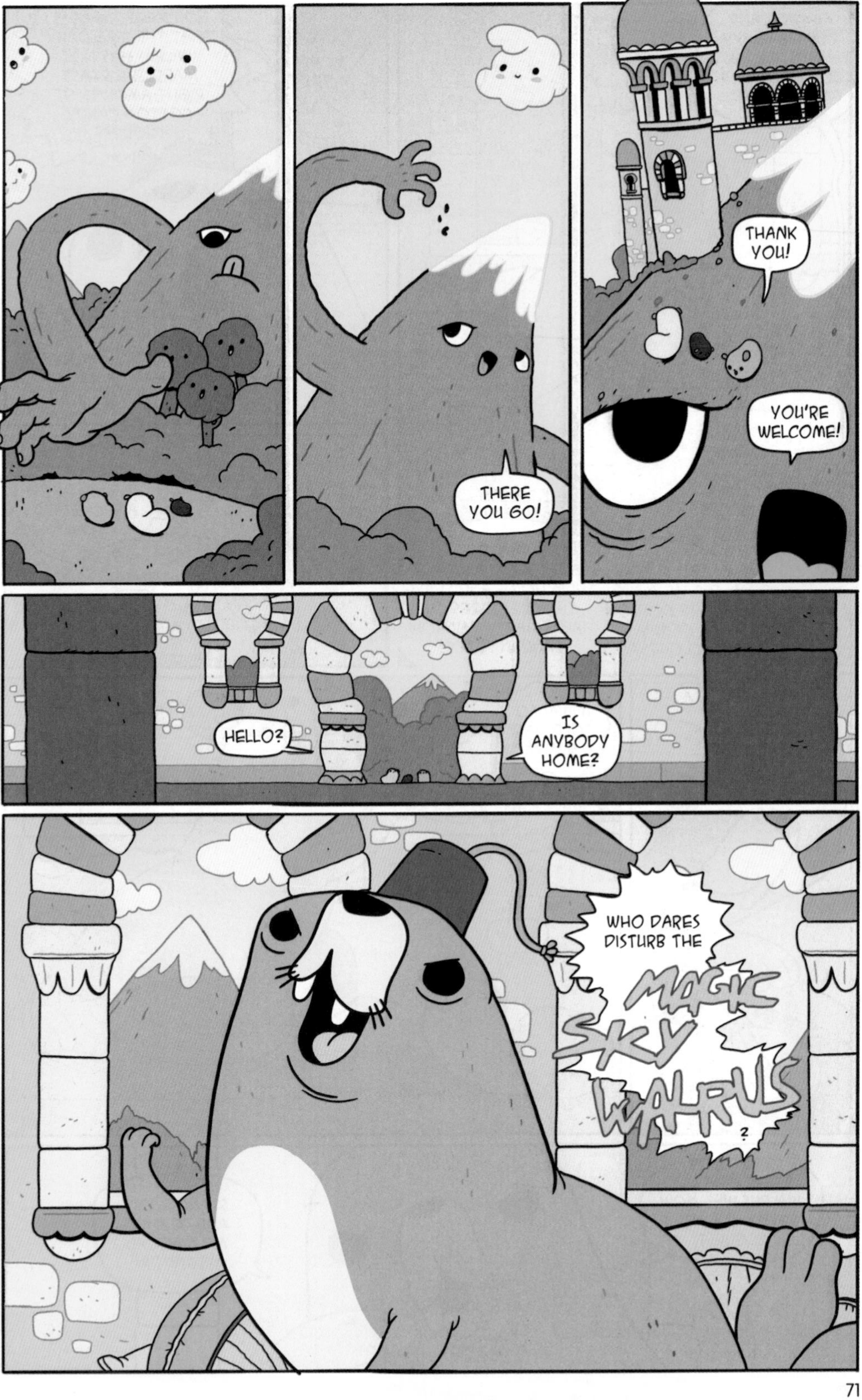
THERE YOU GO!
THANK YOU!
YOU'RE WELCOME!
HELLO?
IS ANYBODY HOME?
WHO DARES DISTURB THE
MAGIC SKY WALRUS
?

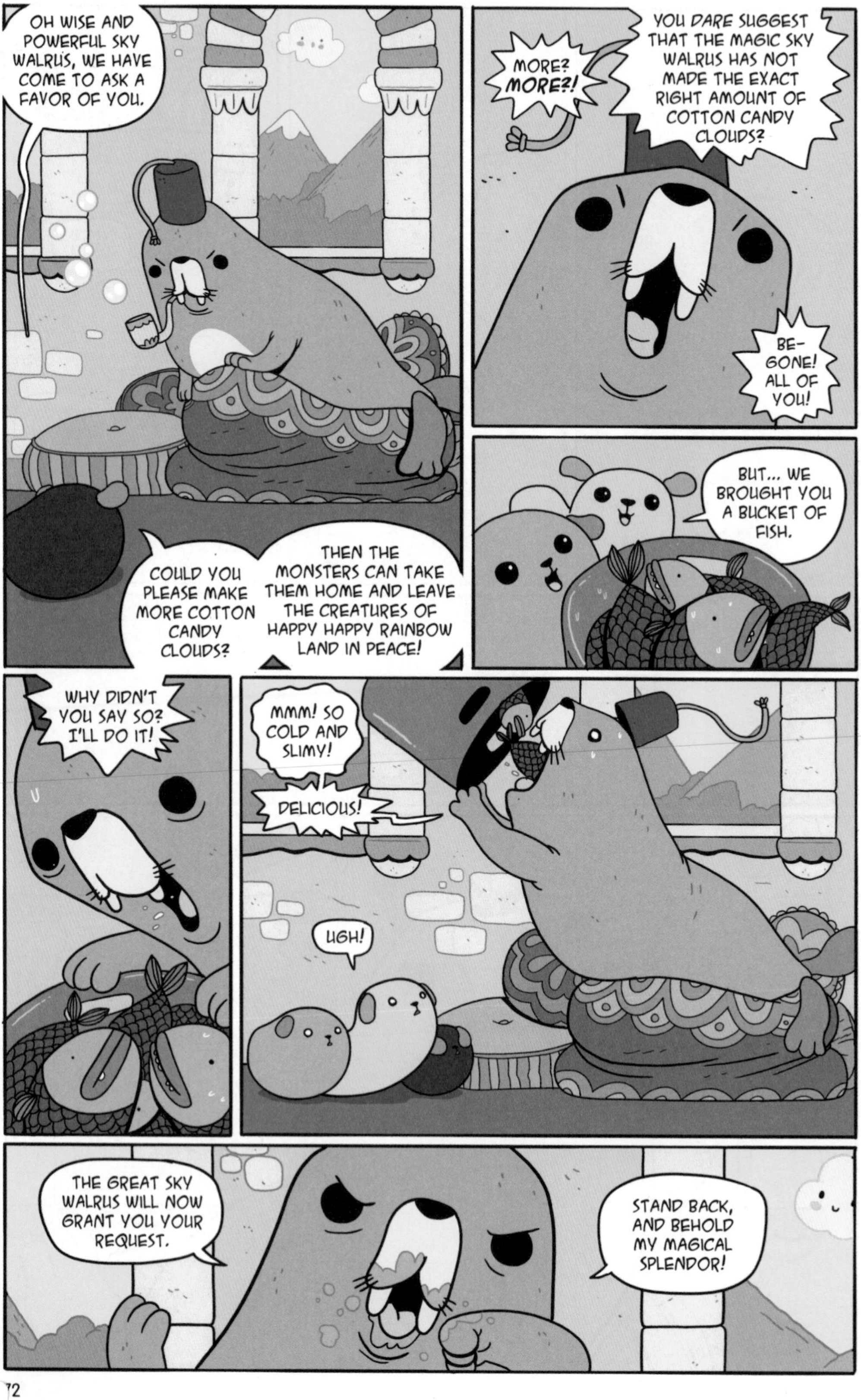
OH WISE AND POWERFUL SKY WALRUS, WE HAVE COME TO ASK A FAVOR OF YOU.
COULD YOU PLEASE MAKE MORE COTTON CANDY CLOUDS?
THEN THE MONSTERS CAN TAKE THEM HOME AND LEAVE THE CREATURES OF HAPPY HAPPY RAINBOW LAND IN PEACE!
MORE? MORE?!
YOU DARE SUGGEST THAT THE MAGIC SKY WALRUS HAS NOT MADE THE EXACT RIGHT AMOUNT OF COTTON CANDY CLOUDS?
BE-GONE! ALL OF YOU!
BUT... WE BROUGHT YOU A BUCKET OF FISH.
WHY DIDN'T YOU SAY SO? I'LL DO IT!
MMM! SO COLD AND SLIMY!
DELICIOUS!
UGH!
THE GREAT SKY WALRUS WILL NOW GRANT YOU YOUR REQUEST.
STAND BACK, AND BEHOLD MY MAGICAL SPLENDOR!

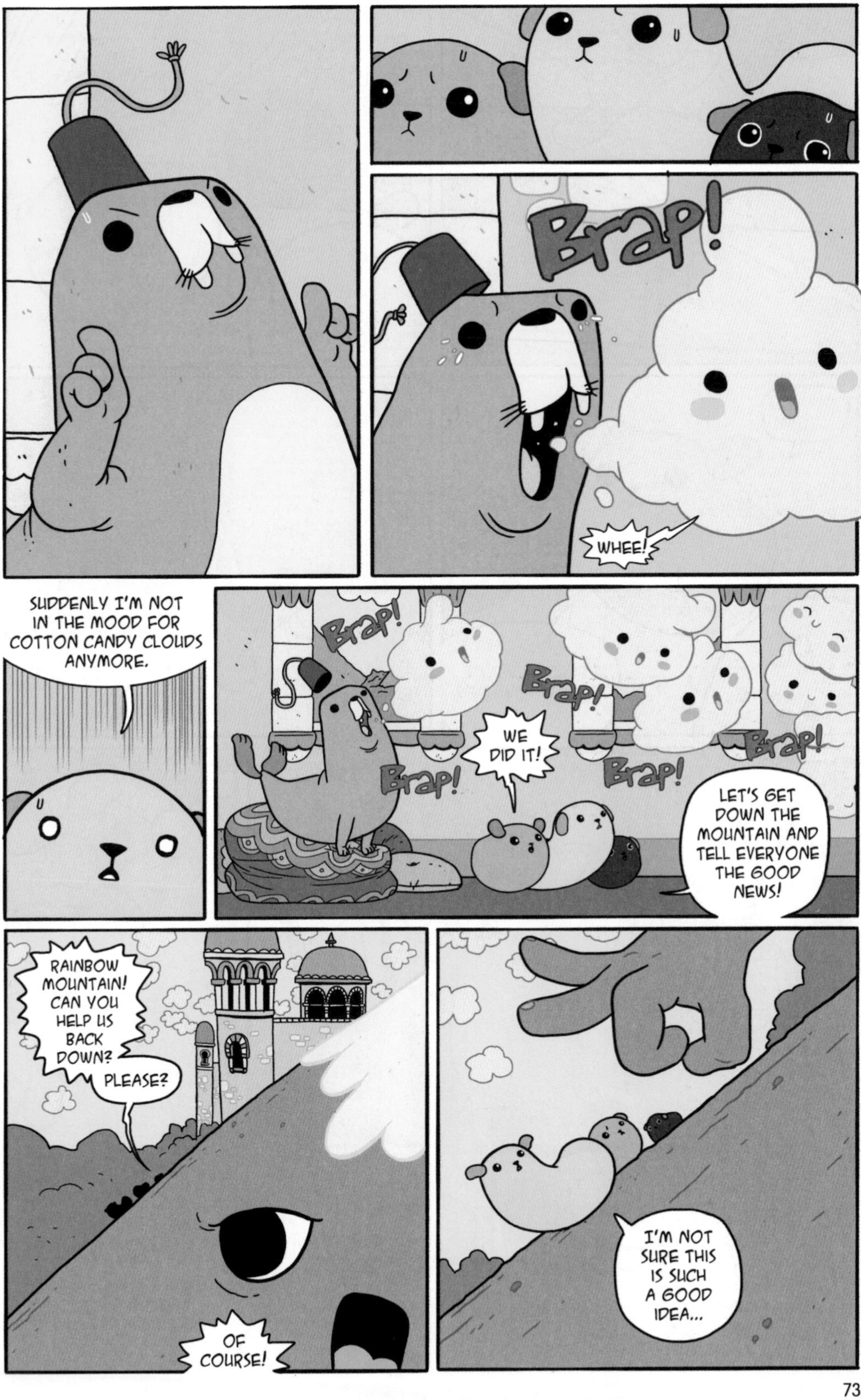
BRAP!
WHEE!
SUDDENLY I'M NOT IN THE MOOD FOR COTTON CANDY CLOUDS ANYMORE.
BRAP!
BRAP!
WE DID IT!
BRAP!
BRAP!
BRAP!
LET'S GET DOWN THE MOUNTAIN AND TELL EVERYONE THE GOOD NEWS!
RAINBOW MOUNTAIN! CAN YOU HELP US BACK DOWN?
PLEASE?
OF COURSE!
I'M NOT SURE THIS IS SUCH A GOOD IDEA...

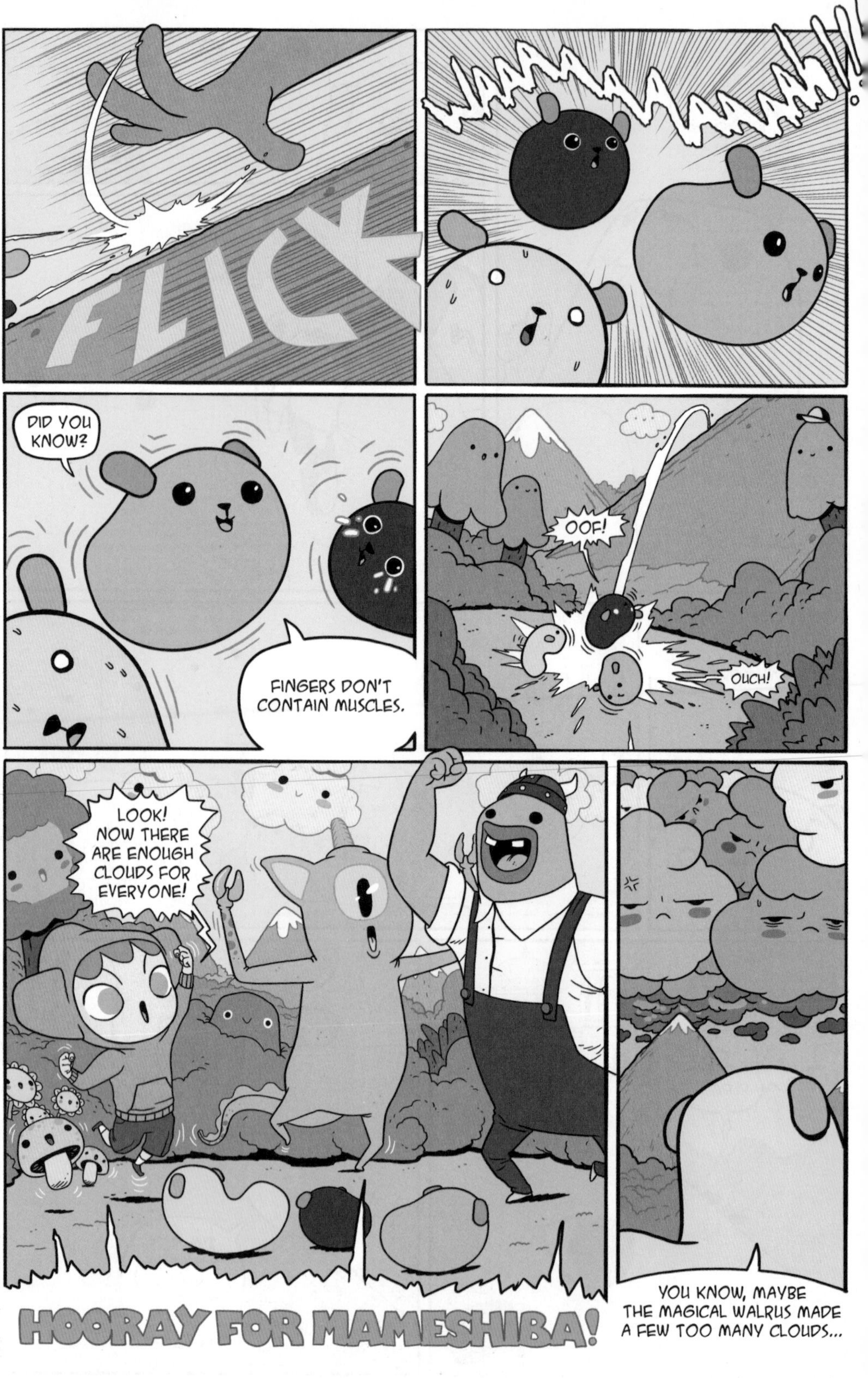
FLICK
WAAAAAAAAAH!!!
DID YOU KNOW?
FINGERS DON'T CONTAIN MUSCLES.
OOF!
OUCH!
LOOK! NOW THERE ARE ENOUGH CLOUDS FOR EVERYONE!
HOORAY FOR MAMESHIBA!
YOU KNOW, MAYBE THE MAGICAL WALRUS MADE A FEW TOO MANY CLOUDS...

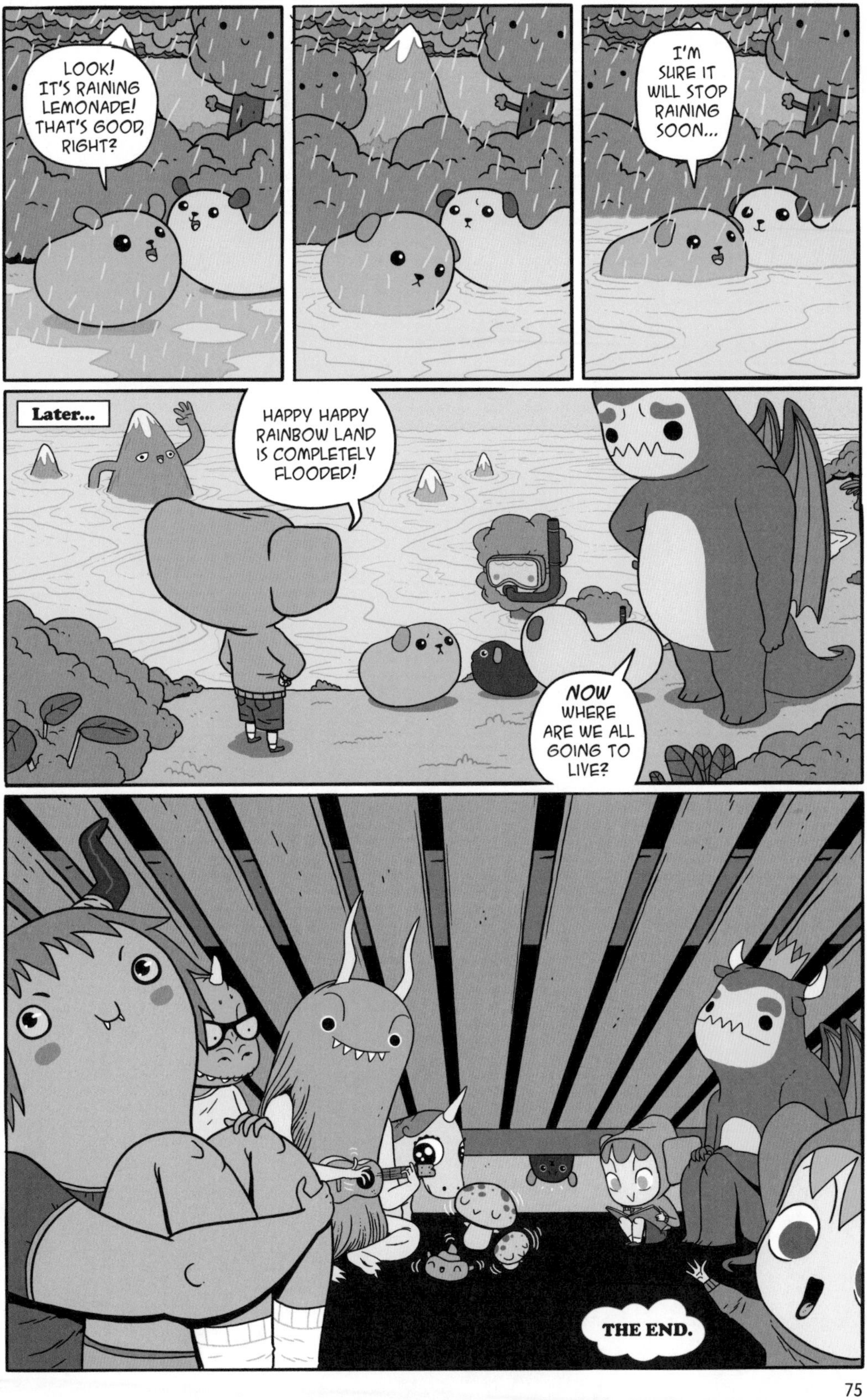
LOOK! IT'S RAINING LEMONADE! THAT'S GOOD, RIGHT?
I'M SURE IT WILL STOP RAINING SOON...
Later...
HAPPY HAPPY RAINBOW LAND IS COMPLETELY FLOODED!
NOW WHERE ARE WE ALL GOING TO LIVE?
THE END.

mameshiba

We Could Be HEROES!

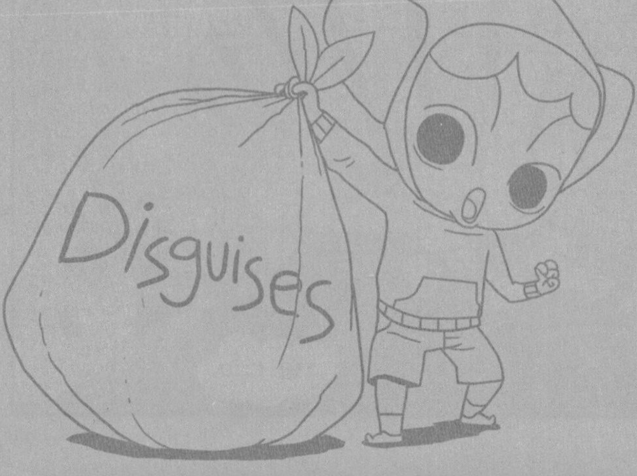
Disguises

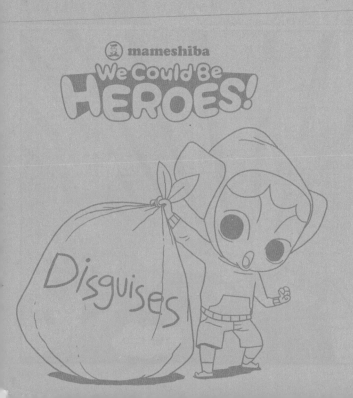

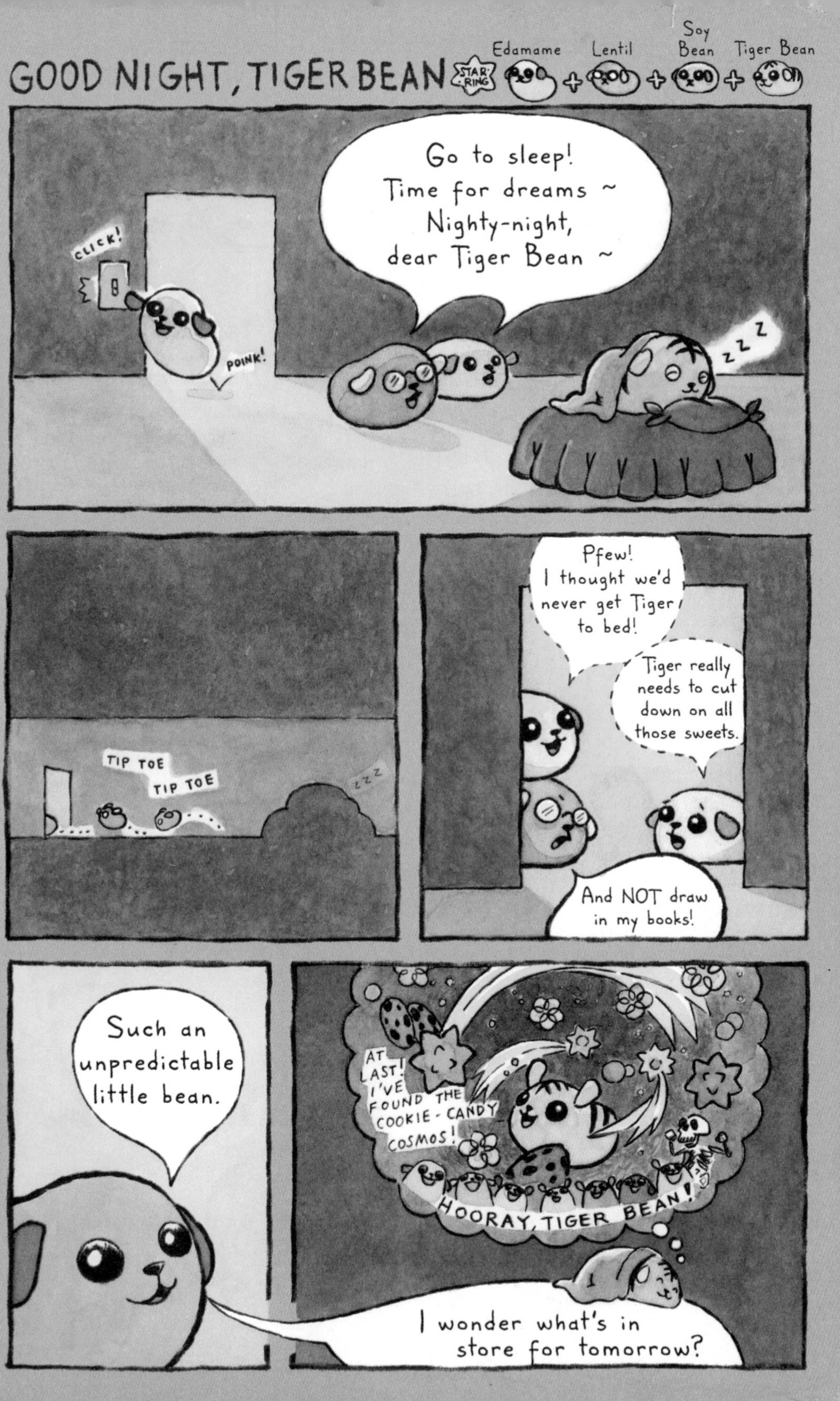
GOOD NIGHT, TIGER BEAN
STARRING
Edamame
Lentil
Soy Bean
Tiger Bean
CLICK!
POINK!
Go to sleep! Time for dreams ~ Nighty-night, dear Tiger Bean ~
Z Z Z
TIP TOE
TIP TOE
Z Z Z
Pfew! I thought we'd never get Tiger to bed!
Tiger really needs to cut down on all those sweets.
And NOT draw in my books!
Such an unpredictable little bean.
AT LAST! I'VE FOUND THE COOKIE-CANDY COSMOS!
HOORAY, TIGER BEAN!
I wonder what's in store for tomorrow?

james turner

started making comics as soon as he was first able to hold a pencil and has been spouting a nonsensical whirlwind of monsters, robots and talking vegetables ever since. His acclaimed web comic *The Unfeasible Adventures of Beaver and Steve* won tens of thousands of followers online, and his anthropomorphic crime fighting team "The Super Animal Adventure Squad" appeared weekly in the pages of the children's comic the DFC. He has sworn that he will not stop making comics until every bizarre character, every unfeasible adventure, and every terrible pun has been uncovered. But he might stop for a bit if someone offers him a biscuit.

jorge monlongo

Monlongoshiba's natural habitat is Madrid, Spain. It eats all sorts of things and likes to sleep late. It can sometimes be seen drawing comic books, illustrating books or painting, but usually it just likes hanging out and being lazy. To learn more about Monlongoshiba, visit **monlongo.com**.

lark pien

is an indie cartoonist from Oakland, California. She has published many comics and is the colorist for Printz winner *American Born Chinese*. Her characters Long Tail Kitty and Mr. Elephanter have been adapted into children's books. She holds the world's tiniest rainbow, which is way heavier than it looks. **larkpien.blogspot.com**

Original Mameshiba characters created and designed by:

Sukwon Kim

Original Mameshiba art direction by:

Shoko Watanabe

Starring in their **first-ever** graphic novel, Mameshiba are on the Loose!

Here's **everything** you ever wanted to know about **Mameshiba**!

It's cold and snowy and Mameshiba are ready to play. **You can join in the fun!**

There's lots more Mameshiba to LOVE!

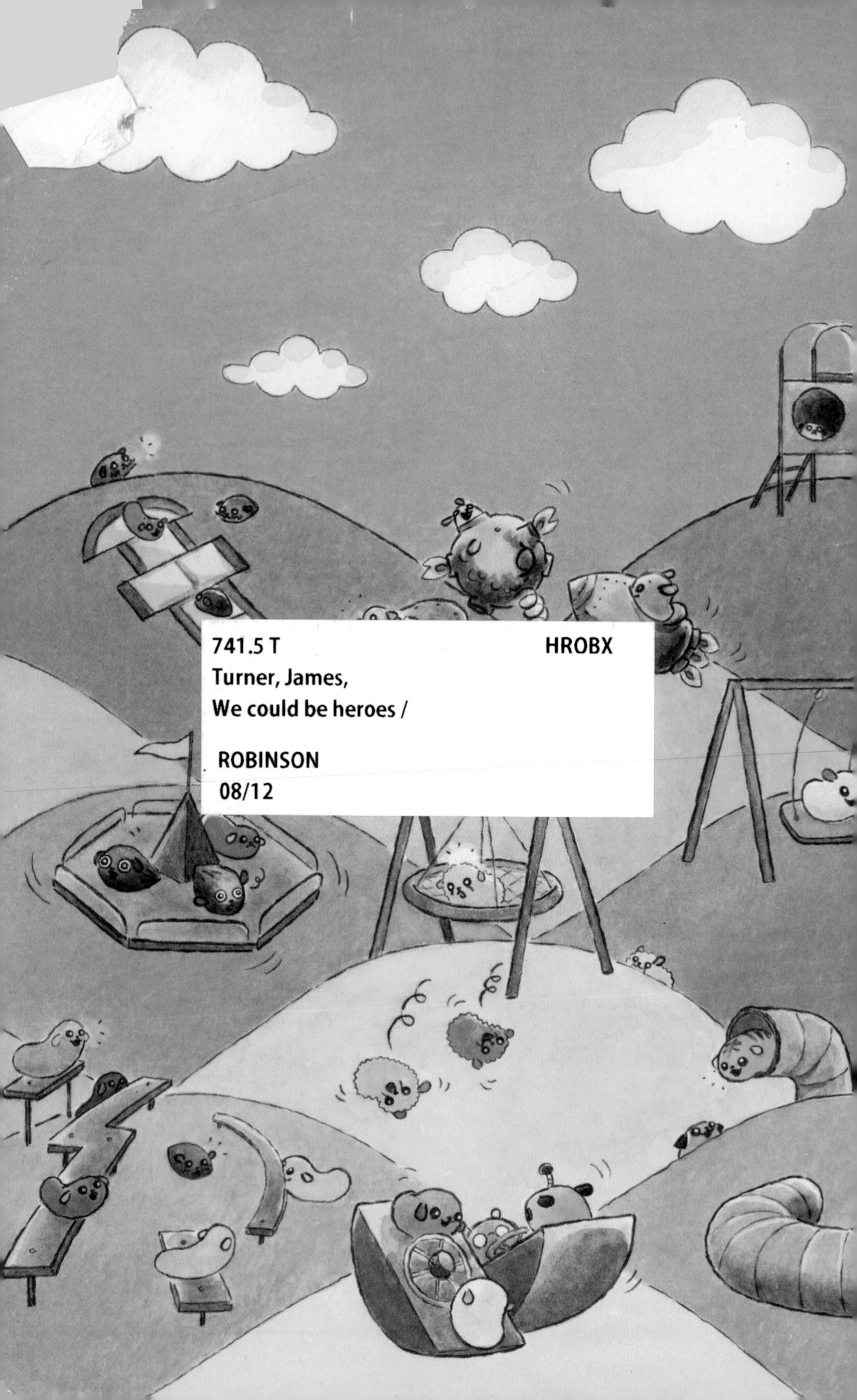